I0679844

I AM THE OIL OF THE ENGINE OF THE WORLD

Stories by Jared Yates Sexton

Praise for Jared Yates Sexton's
The Hook and the Haymaker

"As I worked through Jared Sexton's new short story collection, *The Hook and the Haymaker*, I was reminded of the satisfaction I'd get from listening to a new album and discovering that every song was good; my purchase hadn't been the trap set by the catchy hook of a couple singles. This collection of twenty-three stories, averaging about eight pages each, is the short story equivalent of rock 'n' roll's Exile on Main Street.

--Al Kratz, *the spark*

"Sexton wields reliably tight language to tell these stories of men and women questioning their own happiness (or lack thereof). His sentences are tough instruments, his characters sharp vessels of colloquial—but never stereotypical—speech. He writes in his standard style, without quotation marks, so you'll read carefully and watch closely the rising and falling of the sentences, the dialogue meeting description. There's a kind of effortless rhythm at work, a blending of his prose and his characters' voices."

--Chase Burke, *Atticus Review*

"Sexton's writing is strongest through the characters he develops. Each story captures the essence of the characters whether it be through action or spot-on dialogue that not only reveals specific cultural quirks, but also moves the story forward—a skill many writers lack."

--Julie Demoff-Larson, *Blotterature*

"Sexton's newest collection of twenty-three stories offers a striking example of working-class prose squarely in the vein of Raymond Carver."

--Edmund Zagorin, *The Los Angeles Review*

I AM THE OIL OF THE ENGINE OF THE WORLD

Split Lip Press

I Am the Oil of the Engine of the World © 2016, Jared Yates Sexton. All rights reserved. No part of this book may be used or reproduced without consent from the author or publisher except in the case of brief quotations appropriated for use in articles and reviews.

Published by Split Lip Press
333 Sinkler Road
Wyncote, PA 19095
www.splitlippress.com
www.splitlipmagazine.com

ISBN: 978-0-9909035-6-7

Cover design by Jared Yates Sexton

ACKNOWLEDGMENTS

Some stories have previously appeared in the following publications: You Are But A Pilgrim Venturing To A Strange And Honest Land in *Cleaver Magazine*, New and Better Things in *Dark Sky Magazine*, My Beauty Is So Heavy It Could Crush The Whole of the World in *Fringe Magazine*, Alone, Ypsilanti in *Neon Magazine*, The Only Reason I Got To Be Civilized in *Monkeybicycle*, I Am The Oil of the Engine of the World in *Metazen*, The Hatred In Their Eyes, The Cruelty In Their Hearts in *NANOFiction*, Jennifer Aniston Comes To Stay Awhile in *Punchnel's*, Habit Yourself to the Dazzle of the Light in *Sundog Lit,* On The Empire City in *Crossed-Out Magazine*, Mr. Wimbledon in *WhiskeyPaper*, A Monument For The Dead in *Metazen*, The Death of Second Person in *The Newer York*, Mercy, Gift and Rapture in *Monkeybicycle*, I Want You To Know I Was Here in *Wyvern Lit*, All That Breathes and Crawls in *Stymie*, Carry What You Can Kill in *Lockjaw Magazine*, The Moment Before The Earth Was Destroyed, and Everything That Blossoms in *Cheap Pop Lit*.

ACKNOWLEDGMENTS

CONTENTS

THIS BOOK IS FOR

Shakespeare

YOU ARE BUT A PILGRIM VENTURING TO A STRANGE AND HONEST LAND

On the cab ride in the driver turned and said, Did you know Hope and Despair are sister and brother and you their distant cousin? We were driving over a bridge. Snow was falling and people were trudging down the walk, holding newspapers over their heads.

I'm sorry, I said. I'd been watching the people. What did you say?

I said, he repeated, that Hope and Despair are sister and brother and you their distant cousin.

For some reason I thought over my family tree to see if there was any truth. I was an only child though, the offspring of two miserably matched people who would've still hated one another had they been alive. The only glimpse of hope in my whole lineage was a cousin who had scored well on his Naval test and was chained to the belly of a submarine in the Pacific.

I'm not sure I understand, I said.

It's an easy mistake, the driver said. He was still turned around, his head framed by the glass separating us, his hands busy with the wheel. Most think they're abstract concepts. States of mind. Tricks of brain chemistry. But I'm here to tell you, he said, that they are very real and they are very concerned with you.

From his glove box he pulled a laminated flyer no bigger than a bookmark. I took it with hesitation and studied the print. The first sentence said DID YOU KNOW HOPE AND DESPAIR ARE SISTER AND BROTHER AND YOU THEIR DISTANT COUSIN? There was a picture at the top of two people tugging a rope. There was a woman and a man and they looked like hieroglyphic people who had been locked in eternal struggle.

Those are your cousins, the driver said. The pretty one is Hope. The ugly one Despair.

I looked at Hope and her snake-like locks of dark hair. Despair had a nest of scars racing down his sharp-angled cheek.

Still paying no attention to the road or the crowd of cars he was weaving through, he said, What you didn't know was that you had been locked in a constant family feud. Fought over by a universe as petty and emotional as yourself.

On the back of the laminated flyer was a phone number. Below it a question - WOULD YOU LIKE TO JOIN THE FAMILY?

What's The Family? I said.

The Family, the driver said, is our humble attempt to understand the greater struggle. To find our kin. To commiserate among the likeminded and the frightened.

We were at the airport. The cab had parked itself at the curb leading into the main terminal. The driver was still there with his head poking through the divider. He was smiling, but not. He was grimacing, but not. I told him I didn't have any money.

That's fine, he said.

I said, It's a very strange time in my life.

That's fine, he said.

I said, I'm sorry, but I have a plane to catch.

After scrabbling out of the cab I collected my own bag from the trunk and carried it into the terminal. It was midday and throngs of people choked the space. Everywhere there was someone. They were pushing past one another, holding each other close, screaming into their phones, buying flowers by the ticket stand. I found myself at the counter. I slammed my information on the desk and demanded my boarding pass.

I'm in a hurry, I said.

That's fine, the ticket officer said. She had straight black hair and a crooked tooth in front.

It's a very strange time in my life, I said.

Isn't it for everyone? she said and typed at her keys.

I had to get back to my wife. She'd called the night before from Atlanta and said that the city had begun vibrating. She said she opened up the window to our loft and leaned out and listened. She said it sounded to her like all of the city, all of the towering buildings and beeping cars and hustling people and clanging restaurants, had whispered to her to jump, to fly out of the window and onto the pavement below.

You're in seat 24F, the ticket officer said and handed me my pass.

Wonderful, I said. Thank you, I said.

Listen, she said. Did you know Hope and Despair are sister and brother and you their distant cousin?

What? I said.

Listen, she said and started again.

I have to go, I said.

Security next and I begged my way to the front. Some of the people in line were happy to let me through and others grumbled and yelled and spat. I shoved my shoes and belt and bag through the x-ray machine and walked through the gate. The alarm went off though and a man with security pulled me and my goods to the side.

We need to check you further, he said.

I'm running late for my flight, I said.

That's fine, he said. This will only take a moment.

He waved a wand over my chest and arms and down the back of my legs and then the front. Sir, he said, do you have any metal implants?

Implants? I said.

Pins, he said. Needles. Artificial joints or valves?

No, I said. Nothing of the like.

Good, he said. He touched a button on the wand. You know, he said, the struggle continues whether you are aware of it or not.

The struggle? I said.

Hope is the oldest sibling, he said. She was born in a meadow on a sunlit day. Her mother and father stroked her hair while she cooed and squirmed. Despair came a month later in the midst of a flood that destroyed an entire civilization. The mother was aloft on a makeshift raft and pushed him into the world as all of the bloated animals and peoples bobbed by. She died as he breathed his first breath.

I looked at the man and asked him why he was telling me this.

Because, he told me, it's nearly time.

I left my shoes and belt and bag and ran barefooted across the floor and to my gate. All around me I could hear people talking to each other and into their machines. Their conversations were vastly different, their tones changing and growing as they continued.

I reached my gate and found a phone near the boarding area. I dialed the numbers to my home and my darling wife answered.

As she picked up she said, It's getting worse.

What is? I said. What's getting worse?

The sound, she said. Outside. You should hear it.

I don't want to hear it, I said. I'm already hearing enough. Honey, I said. Are you all right? It's been a strange day.

I'm fine, she said. I'm better than I've ever been. You should hear it though, you really should.

No, I said. Honey, something's happening.

I have to go, she said. I want to listen some more. I'm going to the window.

Don't, I said. Stay away from the window. I'm boarding the plane. Now. I'll be home before you know it. Don't go to the window, I said, but it was no use. She was gone.

The flight boarded and I settled into seat 24F. I'd broken into a sweat that'd soaked through my shirt and pants. My breath, which had been ragged since the incident in the cab, finally slowed and I closed my eyes and envisioned my wife, my beautiful wife, as she had been before I'd left Atlanta. She'd laid next to me. I'd looked at her and she at me.

We are so lucky, I had said.

We are, she said. The luckiest.

None luckier, I said.

But then, as I was remembering, the memory changed and my darling wife raised herself from the bed and opened the window. She pointed to something in the distance. She turned to me, in the memory, and said, You need to listen.

The plane lifted into the air. No one spoke. The captain never came over the address system. There was silence except for the hiss of air through the vents. Things moved faster. It felt as if we were flying at unimaginable speeds. I turned to the person next to me, the person in 24E, an old woman wearing a sweater with a squirrel on the front. I asked her if something was wrong.

Of course something's wrong, she said. There's always something wrong.

The plane's trajectory increased until we were nearly end over end. No one stirred except for me. No one moved except for me. I looked out the window and saw the ground growing farther and farther away and the pressure in my ears built until I thought the drums might burst. My god, I screamed, my god, enough!

As if on cue the plane slowly leveled out and we were parallel to the ground again. The other passengers turned in their seats and looked at me. I expected them to be angry but they seemed serene in a way I'd never seen before. Then, in unison, they unbuckled their seatbelts and stood hunched over. The flight attendants joined them and crowded the aisles. Behind them, the pilot and first officer. All their faces different but somehow the same. And then, in a moment, a subtle ripple ran across them as if across the surface of a pond.

Did you know, they said together in perfect coordination, that Hope and Despair are sister and brother and you their distant cousin?

Their stare was so intense I had no choice but to look away. Out the window I could see that the landscape was changing somehow. It was warping. Transforming.

What you have seen for so long, they said, is a distraction. Life hidden by a powerless daydream.

I watched a cornfield below rise in a wave and then flatten out like the last breath of a tide. It was then I realized my fellow passengers had me surrounded.

It's time to wake up, they said, their voices still in lockstep, their eyes unblinking. It's time to see the true nature of reality.

The level of the plane changed again and I could feel the force of descent. The pilots were still standing there, their hands lifeless at their sides. I felt the shape of something in my pocket and I found the laminated flyer the driver had given me in the cab. My eyes were drawn to a line at the bottom - YOU ARE BUT A PILGRIM VENTURING TO A STRANGE AND HONEST LAND.

I looked outside. The world glowed now with the tint of a mad and dying sun. Where there had once been Atlanta, with its skyscrapers shouldering up from the concrete, was now a city with glorious temples and glass spires surrounding a smoking cavity of a pit full of rotting and decaying flesh. There were people dancing and making love in the streets and there were people flaying one another.

Welcome home, they said in one voice. Welcome.

NEW AND BETTER THINGS

The Briar Patch Killer struck again last night. It's the first in six months, the return of an era. In his interviews he speaks at length about the pressure, about the attention and how it's changed everything. The television specials. The T-shirts. It's not as pure, not as organic. But something on the outskirts of Topeka must've stirred him.

The first victim was a woman named Marlene Satchings. What a wonderful name. It looked just right in the newspaper headlines. She was beautiful on the nightly news. Curly red hair and full-moon blue eyes. The picture was from her twenty-first birthday party, a cardboard cone hanging nonchalantly off her head and attached by a rubber band that ran beneath her perfect chin. Suspended there forever, twenty-one years old, gone but never forgotten.

For weeks everyone was obsessed with Marlene. Charities sprouted up everywhere, signs saying REMEMBER MARLENE, bumper stickers, web sites and memorials. It was unthinkable, what'd happened. She'd gone for a walk in Kansas one night, to clear her mind a friend said, and was found the next day, stashed away in a briar patch off a trail, by a jogger and his faithful dog. She'd been torn apart. The jogger said it looked like a wild animal had gotten a hold of her. Torn her to shreds. It took weeks to identify her, weeks to put together the pieces, and then, just like that, we had Marlene Satchings and that photograph of her blowing out those birthday candles, wearing her birthday hat, enjoying the last birthday she'd ever have.

Then another. Sandy Something. In Kansas as well. Same curly red hair, same blue eyes, just not as pretty, not as memorable. We didn't swoon over her though, the charities were few and far between. No bumper stickers were sold. The story was less glamorous. She'd been standing outside her house, having a smoke, when disaster struck. The mutilation itself wasn't as extensive. It was as if the Briar Patch Killer himself had been completely unimpressed. The good thing, however, was that it told the country exactly what we wanted to hear, what we had been hoping for, what we'd been praying for. There was a new killer on the loose, one who wasn't afraid to get his hands dirty. One who wasn't afraid to strike and strike with regularity.

Can you believe it? my wife said.

I can't believe it, I said.

Life was hard back then.

It seemed like every day there was an article or a segment on the killings. Expert analysis on when and where he might strike again, why he might be butchering innocent women, where he might be, what walk of life he travelled in, the tools at his disposal. We speculated in our cubicles and over our lunches. On more than one occasion I had a long discussion at a dinner party. The hostess told me she thought the killer was an artist, a man who saw the world as his own personal canvas in which to draw his brush. Her husband, a loan officer, chimed in at one point and said it was all his wife wanted to talk about anymore. This killer and his killings. She shushed him in due order and said she couldn't wait to see the finishing touches.

Three women in three days. Red hair. Blue eyes. Two of them found off of walkways, the other in her very own living room. All of them mutilated, all of them on our television screens, one of them on video, running on a treadmill as if being perpetually chased from here unto eternity, her ponytailed red hair bobbing like a lure. It was all we could talk about. Specials, a rumored feature-length film. Talks of a weekly series dedicated to nothing but the investigation. You started seeing more women with red hair. Women buying blue-tinted contacts. My wife bought the official T-shirts, complete with slogans. ME NEXT. THINK I'LL GO FOR A RUN TONIGHT.

Then, a strange moment. A woman taken down in Milwaukee. Red hair, yes, but not quite as red as the others. Strawberry-blonde maybe. Green eyes. The mess that was her remains not quite the artistic statement we'd all grown used to. The girl, I forget her name now, was average at best. The talk turned to whether or not the killer had lost his edge, whether he was winding down, over the hill, or worse, unchallenged and uninspired. The sloppiness threatened our attention. Someone in New Haven killed a Chinese woman, stuffed her into a suitcase in the bus terminal, and left her by a newsstand. Our attention was divided.

The Briar Patch Killer responded via a letter to the National Broadcast Corporation. They read his words on the Nightly News. The Milwaukee woman had been the victim of a copycat, a rather lackluster counterfeit. The killer promised his vision was pure and true and developing at an acceptable pace. Widespread destruction was imminent, new and better things on the horizon. Within twenty-four hours we would see. We were promised a new killing, this one bigger and greater than the last, a crime we wouldn't soon forget. Stay tuned, he said.

We did and we weren't disappointed. A sorority house at the University of Houston, down the gut of the country, filled with five girls who'd been visited and disposed of with the deftest of touches. The scene, which we saw from the released photographs and investigative video, looked as if it were a new Pollack, a masterpiece no one could deny. Crime reporters were joined by art critics on the programs. The killer's sense of space, they said, was challenged only by the great masters, the artists we hold so dearly in our hearts and consciousness. We should leave this be, one critic said of the house. Never touch it, never clean it up, leave it be for the generations to come. We must think of them, the generations to come.

A thrust of new murders, each one more important than the last. Women cut down in their primes, in the wash of the afternoon sun. Bystanders reporting they were just standing there, drinking a coffee, cleaning their nails, the girl next to them, perched on a stool, legs kicking, humming a tune, carefree, exploding, instantly, the killer moving so fast they didn't catch more than a blur. Trading cards were sold. Movie-of-the-weeks.

I talked to my wife, a beautiful young woman, curly red hair of her own, deep eyes like the sea. I talked to my wife and I asked her what she thought of everything. I'm thrilled every day, she said. Thrilled constantly. Thrilled to the point of boredom. We were sitting at the breakfast table, trading cups of tea and wrinkling the morning paper. There was great unrest in our lives until the killer came. A constant need to yell and run into the night, full-bore, run until there were no more lights and the dark closed in, 'til we'd found ourselves, lungs and legs spent, pushing the border into a neighboring town. After though, we laid in bed, the both of us exhausted from particularly violent bouts of lovemaking, the sweat drying on our skin, she no doubt fantasizing about the killer, me imagining her walking down a dimly-lit path, her exposed skin shining like a beacon for lost ships.

Then we heard he was going to appear live on television, a talent show for adults, a last-chance kind of program where you sang and danced and performed monologues to get fed and have your utilities paid. Of course we tuned in. Everyone did. You could practically feel the gravity of it pulling you into your TV. The show opened with a pair of worn, homeless-looking people, two men doing somersaults across the stage, flaming flares in their hands, bowls of fish balanced on their backs. The crowd looked restless, sitting at their dinner tables, cutting into their steaks and cracking lobster tails to the tune of candlelight. After the performance they showed the killer in silhouette, blacked-out from the world, a graphic labeling him The Briar Patch Killer, To Be Revealed Soon. The host, a short little scamp with gelled-up hair and a holographic bowtie, scampered onstage and hyped the reveal some more, said it was going to be the biggest event in the history of whatever, sang a song he had written for the occasion, and the crowd, halfway through their initial entree, politely clapped and dotted their sweaty faces with napkins. I clapped. My beautiful wife clapped. We were too nervous not to clap. We gripped each other's hands. We sweated. We paced the room.

The time came and there he was, in silhouette. The host's holographic tie shone in the stage lights. Now is the time, he said, and the shadow retreated. My beautiful wife squeezed my knee and said, Oh my god. The sound of three thousand sets of silverware falling on clothed tables. The killer revealed, a middle-aged man with receding hair, normal and unremarkable eyes, a weak chin. He wore a nondescript light jacket, the kind you might find on sale at Sears.

The host, seemingly so shocked by his ordinariness, cut the broadcast. It slunk into a testing pattern, a beep alternating the seconds. We sat in front of the TV all night, hoping it might come back on, hoping the host and the killer would return and the nightmare reversed.

The next day it was all people wanted to discuss at work - how ordinary the killer looked. What kind of fraud was that? someone said to me. Who builds up peoples' expectations and destroys them? Almost everyone seemed to agree. Some though were of the opinion that it made it all the better. He could be anyone, said a friend of mine. That's the point, he said. He could be your neighbor, could be you, could be your father. You never know.

But we need strong character, I said.

We need strong character, my beautiful wife said. A man who can bend the universe to his will and destroy what others might simply be content to hold.

That night, the next night, the talent show re-aired, did the entire thing over. The same homeless men performed, the somersaults, the flares, the fish bowls on their backs, but when they finished they looked almost embarrassed, they peered into the camera with an aw shucks kind of glance and sauntered backstage. The host, with a different holographic tie, came into the spotlight and said he was sorry there'd been such a terrible difficulty the night before, that we could rest assured there'd be no such problem this time around.

And my god there wasn't. My beautiful wife and I sat there and watched the killer revealed again, this time his hair was full and his eyes alight with a kind of sadistic glow, his chin strong and his body enveloped by the same kind of clothes we'd grown accustomed to movie stars and dignitaries wearing to film premiers. He spoke with power, with thrust, as he told us about his plan to dominate life, to take the spark from persons with curly red hair and dark blue eyes and how that might someday transform into something else, another period if you will, but he couldn't predict when or how. We cried, my wife and I, from the excitement and the fear. I ran my hands through her red hair and pressed my face into it. I slipped a curl or two into my mouth and bit down with my teeth and felt the strands slip into my gums.

The killer was everywhere. On the morning shows. Children's shows. Cereal boxes. It went on and on and he killed another half-dozen, split them in two in public, on the buses, in intersections, at dinner parties, a press-event at the White House. Everyday more killer news, as if he was in more than one place. A death in Baltimore in the morning and another, in Guam, at dusk. Sometimes the clouds seemed to take the shape of the killer, the earlier shape, the balding man, the weak man, the ordinary man.

But then, like that, it stopped. No more killings. A drought, they called it. Perhaps he took a break. Perhaps he lacked inspiration. The newspapers rumored he was going on vacation to England, digging up family roots and studying the origins of mass violence. But after a month that didn't seem to be much of an explanation. A month later and we knew it couldn't be true. The killer had left us, we decided, and the newscasters lost their energy, delivered the daily update with a listlessness that bordered on contempt. Businesses closed because workers quit reporting for their shifts. There was a story that some people simply stopped eating, like animals in mourning. My wife, my lovely red-curled wife, went on long walks, wore hardly a stitch on her, and when she returned, close to three or four in the morning, her face was streaked with spent tears and run mascara.

I held her. I spoke into her ear. I twirled my finger in her red hair. In truth, I was restless myself, tired of our love, tired of her loveliness, tired of waiting on the killer to emerge, tired of having to reaffirm that she was beautiful, as beautiful as Marlene Satchings – though she was not – and tired of everyday complacency. Someday, I said to her, to my wife. Someday you and the killer will cross paths.

He's gone, she said. There was defeat in her voice. Sadness I'd never heard before.

He's not, I said. He's reloading. Finding his muse. Preparing even more terrible ways to torture you, to deliver pain and blinding agony.

You only say things you think I want to hear, she said. She grabbed the clock off our nightstand and hurled it tiredly at the wall. It exploded. Its parts, its springs and gears and innards spilled onto the floor. In my exhausted state I thought I could see time pooling into a black puddle.

Then, Topeka. This time, finally, a return to form, a red-haired girl, jogging down a path, her body, her sweet mutilated body, found, get this, in a briar patch. We were sleeping, my wife and I. It was past noon at that point. We'd lost all will to get up in the morning. We'd lost our jobs and were simply waiting for the mortgage company to come calling, the power to flicker off, the last vestiges of our lives to slip and flutter away. The phone rang. Once, twice, three, four, five, six, seven times. Everyone wanting us to know the killer was back, the killing had begun. Her mom, my mom, friends, cousins, strangers who, in their excitement, had dialed our number on accident. Outside our window the children were lining up in the streets for an impromptu parade. They were painting themselves in red paint and artificial gore. The parents stabbing each other with real and plastic knives, biting themselves on the shoulders, gnawing on their fingers.

My wife launched out of bed as if fired from a gun. She ran into the closet and I was right behind. We found her jogging clothes, the sports bra and tight bottoms, tube socks and sprinting shoes. In a fury of hands and feet and soft parts we dressed her and combed her hair and painted her face in makeup. She got her curling iron out and curled her already massive red curls. We cried and kissed with our tongues and practically fell over each other on our way to the front door. There's hope we said, the maddening cries and screams of our neighbors all around us. Go find him, I said. Thank god, she said. There's still hope, she said. There's still hope, I said.

ALONE, YPSILANTI

I have this dream. This dream where everything goes wrong. It all goes wrong and my teeth fall out. They crack and break and fall out of my head. I'll be talking to someone – my girlfriend, my mom, my dentist – and it starts. I'm talking and then I'm watching my teeth fall out. I close my mouth and try and hold them back but they rush out like a waterfall, a sea of white teeth vomiting out of me.

·

I always wake up. I'm in a bed under my comforter, in my bedroom, in my house. In Michigan. In my girlfriend's arms. I scream and touch my teeth to be sure. You had the dream again, my girlfriend says. I did, I say. I was in a jungle and running from a gorilla. Your teeth fell out, my girlfriend says. All over the canopy, I say. They fell in a pile and the pile grew until it was a mountain. A mountain of teeth, my girlfriend says. A mountain of teeth, I say.

·

Over breakfast we discuss the dream. My girlfriend and me. I stir my coffee while she scoops the heart out of a grapefruit. I'm still frightened, I tell her. You should be, she says. I read in a magazine it means you have something to say, she says. Something difficult. I take a drink but can't taste anything. I put my cup down and try my teeth again. They are all sturdy, good fine teeth. My dentist tells me there's nothing to worry about. He tells me I am a wonderful specimen.

.

My mom and I shop at the mall at stores with age-appropriate blouses and slacks. You need rest, she says to me. She is searching through a bin of discount costume jewelry. You're tired, she says. You're worn, she says. Maybe, I say. You're too worried about your career, she says. What career? I say. I don't have a career, I say.

I don't have a career.

.

My dentist, so happy to see me. His staff of buxom nurses always close to his side. My son, he says as he puts me in his chair and places a bib around my neck. One of his nurses, a blonde with curls the size of racecar shocks, fumbles with his belt while another, a short redhead, massages his fingers with oils and stones. The exam begins and he coos and the nurses coo. What teeth, he says. What wonderful, lovely teeth. I want to take pictures, he says. I want to hang pictures of your teeth from every wall in my house.

.

A television commercial tells me I am not in a dream. A lawyer in his office, selling class-action lawsuits. His hair perfect. Gold watches on his wrist. You are not dreaming, he says. This world is real, he says. You are real, he says. And then more about class action lawsuits. Hotlines and fine print.

•

A presentation. My girlfriend and me sitting in our living room, on our couch, drinking glasses we haven't owned in ages. Pay attention to the graph, she says. The peaks and valleys tell the entire story. Here is the height of our love. She points to a wonderful swell in the past. And here it is, she says, pointing to a rot-colored line that runs to the bottom of the poster board. This is today, she says. This is where my love has ceased, she says. I think I'm dreaming, I say. You're not dreaming, she says.

•

A restaurant, a table in the front, by the windows, my mom and me watching the cars pass. A lady next to us is discussing an explosion in the sky. Limbs littering the street. My mom breaks a bone on her plate and sucks the marrow until there is no marrow to suck. I'm marrying your father again, she says. I think I'm asleep, I say. I think I'm dreaming, I say. You're not dreaming, she says. Her hands glisten with sweat. I'm marrying your father again, she says. But Dad's been dead for eight years, I say. No, she says. He's only been resting.

•

The nurses prepare bowls of water and milk and sing with the voice of a tight-hinged door. A thousand radios on every shelf of my dentist's office, all tuned to the same static-filled station. Your teeth, he says. He's taking pictures with a camera the size of a station wagon, the nurses strumming his chest. A hammer in his apron, a bucket at his side. He slams the head against my teeth and they shatter. My dentist fills his fist with them and swings again. The nurses take their turns. My mouth filled. My lap filled. The bucket and floor filled. The room filled and my dentist and his nurses swimming through a white sea. I'm dreaming, I say to myself. My dentist, through the waves, his head the size of a mad whale's, the nurses like barnacles suckling from his giant whale teats. You're not dreaming, he bellows. I promise you, you are not dreaming.

And I'm inclined to believe.

I AM THE OIL OF THE ENGINE OF THE WORLD

I made my first million at seventeen designing a computer program that managed a household budget. If you came in under a specific amount a trumpet sounded in triumph. Come in over and a violin played a particularly sad tune. That million went toward a whole host of things, a car, a big house in the suburbs, a security system that separated me from the world. It also went into development. The billion came from an application that, when used, seeped into your world and took your relevant information. That information was sold to the highest bidder and I found myself flush with more cash than I could ever hope to spend.

Nowadays I watch television. I watch so much television it would alarm you. In the morning it's *The Today Show*, segments about new gadgets and trends. Self-propelled lawn mowers and self-cleaning toothbrushes. When the hostess in the pretty dress takes the toothbrush in her dainty little hand, when she opens her mouth wide, sheepishly grinning, and sticks the brushed end into her jaw, that's when I pull down my pajama bottoms and jack off as fast as I can. If I do it right I can jizm before she's done. Some days I rush into the bathroom and clean myself off with a wet washrag, but others, when I'm feeling particularly bored or lazy, I sit there on my couch and let the jizz harden on my belly. I've made it all the way to *Family Feud* before without getting up and cleaning my belly off with a wet washrag.

When you do everything you get tired of everything. You wouldn't think it was the case but it's true. You charter a jet down to Florida or the Caribbean enough times and it's just like getting your teeth cleaned. You fly out to California to see the sun set a second time and it's no better than making a sandwich. Sometimes I think all I want to do is sit there on my couch and jack off to *The Today Show*. That's the only thing that makes me happy anymore.

I get sidetracked. I walked downtown the other day and found my way into this boutique. There weren't mannequins there. God no. There were people, beautiful people, beautiful people paid to wear the clothes and look beautiful. One of them, a beautiful boy with cheekbones like marble, was wearing a three-piece suit with pinstripes. He looked so good I bought myself the same suit. I bought three suits, not a one of them different. The girl behind the counter asked if I really wanted three of them and I told her yes, three of those same suits, and charge me full price, none of this clearance bullshit. She rang it all up and the model smiled and I smiled and while I was smiling and looking at him smiling I noticed another boy, this one just as handsome as the first one, a few feet past him. He looked different, beautiful still but different, and it took me a whole minute just to put my finger on why. He was wearing a three-piece suit, much like the ones I had just purchased, but atop his head, his well-maintained head, a black bowler hat.

Now, I'd seen bowler hats before. I'd seen them in movies and in plays and when I went to Wales sometimes, for something to do, I saw the men there wear bowler hats out for dinner. It had never occurred to me to buy a bowler hat before but right then it really seemed like something I should do. So I did. I grabbed that bowler hat right off the second handsome model and I put it atop my own head and looked in the mirror. It looked like it had always been there, like I'd been born to wear a bowler hat atop my head.

I went home. I turned on the television. *The Today Show* wasn't on but I pulled up my DVR, which was filled to the brim with recorded episodes. I found my favorite clip, the one where the hostess in the pretty dress is making pancakes with a famous celebrity chef. They're standing on the set and mixing up a bowl of batter. I take the opportunity--I have all of this timed, mind you-- and strip off the three-piece suit I've just bought and toss it on the floor. I'm sitting there on my couch, my thingee bobbing up and down like a fishing pole, my new fancy three-piece suit in a pile by my feet, the bowler hat perched right there atop my head. It was all too much. I couldn't handle it. I jizmed right then and right there, even before the hostess in the pretty dress poured that batter onto a stainless griddle. I jizmed so hard and so fast that I shook and the bowler hat fell off my head and onto the couch beside me.

Ecstasy.

The rest of the day I spent on the couch, watching old clips of *The Today Show*. I waited until the feeling had passed and started again. I timed it so well that I knew just when the hostess in the pretty dress was about to take that big wooden spoon of hers, the one she'd used to stir the pancake batter, and when she was about to drip it onto the stainless griddle. I experimented. Sometimes I'd wear that bowler hat and sometimes I'd take it off and rest it on the arm of the couch. I even went into my bedroom and got a standing mirror and set it up next to the television. I wanted to see what it looked like when I jacked off while watching *The Today Show*.

That took up maybe a week of my time. It drove me mad. Whenever I wasn't sitting in front of the television and watching *The Today Show* and wearing my bowler hat and jacking off it was all I could think about. I had meetings and conference calls. I'd get so worked up, sitting in a boardroom with my bowler hat right there on my head, I'd make up some excuse to leave. Then I'd come right back home and plop on the couch. You know what happened next.

During a video call one night I realized a manager of one of my seemingly infinite accounts couldn't see below my neck. I realized he could only see my smiling face and that bowler hat. It was too much to stand. I turned on the television and found an episode where the hostess was wearing her pretty dress and showing a new type of paint that could be erased like chalk. She used her dainty little hand and got a brush full of the paint and she started painting a giant white wall. The strokes she used were perfect and careful and I returned to the video call and talked to the manager of one of my many accounts and under the eye of the computer screen I jacked off and jizmed all over my hand and legs and never missed a beat talking about my investments.

I have so much money. You would be so impressed.

I went for a walk the other day and saw my money moving. It moves like blood through veins, through arteries, through the body of the world at-large. The lights are mine, the sky is mine, the woman standing at the mailbox, looking like the hostess but without the pretty dress, she is mine as well and I walked over to her with my bowler hat and said hello and she looked away and I asked if she liked my bowler hat and she wouldn't say anything. Don't you like my bowler hat, I asked her. Don't you like it?

No one wears bowler hats. No one but me. I paid a few million to start a campaign. Bowler hats for everyone. For men. For women. For the poor. For pets even. I want to walk around and feel like my thingee, hard like a bomb. I want to feel the blood pump through me like a goddamn missile. I paid a public relations firm four million dollars, that covered their services and all the bowler hats needing bought. They handed them out. Gave away coupons. Everyone wearing bowler hats. Everyone walking around and my thingee beating like the heart of a goddamn giant.

Jesus fucking christ.

Out there in the streets it's a goddamn orgy. I watch the people walking and those hats bouncing and I just think my god, I am the oil of the engine of the world. The banks are full of me and they rise up like hard-ons, like thingees set on granite. I walk into banks and take out millions just to put it in other banks. I leave bowler hats everywhere. Vagrants wearing bowler hats. I get on a plane and leave the city and go to another city, and bowler hats. Models and pissants wearing bowler hats. Hello bowler hat, I say. Hello bowler hat, they say.

Look at me run.

In one day I went outside and flew to Utah for no reason and flew back home. The mountains were alive with snow and mist and the trends take so long to get there but my god my waitress this morning, looking just like the hostess with the pretty dress, she handed me my coffee at the diner, she put the cream and sugar on my plate, and gave me a pat of butter for my bread. She unfolded a napkin and placed it ever so daintily on my lap and by then I'm sure she could feel my thingee trying to escape from the trousers of my three-piece suit, and then, like magic, like the breath of god, the brims of our bowler hats touched and I jizmed right there, right there in the diner, and she said there's a big boy, and the bowler hat fell off my head and onto the floor and she picked it up and flashed me her secret smile.

I went home, first thing. I couldn't take it anymore. Everywhere I went I was jizming and felt like I was losing myself. The man I sat next to on the plane wore, you guessed it, his very own bowler hat, the magazine in his lap proclaiming that bowler hats were the new thing, a family full of bowler hats, their picnic laid out before them, a meadow of bowler hats, the hostess with the pretty dress in the background, a bowler hat, traipsing through a forest, her very own family of bowler hats, behind them, bowler hats, behind them, you know, my god, you know.

In my house I sit and think. I plot my next move. The television plays nothing anymore except for *The Today Show*. The hostess in the pretty dress is showing a device that allows your bowler hat to wear a bowler hat. The inventor wears three bowler hats and the weatherman five. They shake hands and the hostess in the pretty dress takes a bowler hat and runs her fingers around the edges and looks into the camera. She takes the bowler hat and places it, ever so slowly, on top of the other bowler hat, and in that smile, that damned dirty smile, I know that she knows just what she's done.

THE ONLY REASON I GOT TO BE CIVILIZED

I'm motherfucking Superman, Bower yelled from the back of the bar. He picked up a chair and bashed it to bits against a Budweiser sign on the wall. He was in rare form.

All things considered, Teddy said at the bar, I'm being a very patient man.

Sitting next to him, looking scared-sober and just scared in general, was Jeff Keene. He was staring past Teddy, at Bower's rampage, and stroking the sweat from his untouched beer. Nobody said you wasn't, he said to Teddy. Very patient, he said.

It's just hard to stay that way, Teddy said and took a swig of the Jim Beam in his hand. Something like this happens and it just tests the shit out of your patience.

Bower, still in the back, broke a mirror and collected the shattered pieces. He drug them over his muscled arms and drew great rivers of blood. I'm gonna kill tonight, he coughed. Kill, kill, kill.

Maybe, Teddy said. Maybe you will and maybe you won't. All depends on what William here has to say about it.

You know I'm a buddy of yours, Jeff said. Always have been.

That's a fact, Teddy said.

Your pop and my pop used to thick as thieves, Jeff said, wiping perspiration from his eyes.

Used to get their ball bats and go looking for trouble, Teddy said. Went down to the tracks and cleaned out all the tramps and undesirables.

Bower was in a rage. He smeared blood across his face and was beating a night-black bruise into his chest.

Fella like Bower, Teddy said, would've fit in a whole lot better back in those days. Back when there was honor and morality.

I promise, Jeff pleaded. I don't know nothing 'bout those pictures. Where they come from, what they look like, who's giving them out.

I wish you wouldn't say that, Teddy said. The truth is so much more desirable. He slugged back his glass and drained the Jim Beam. Hey Bower, he said. Show Jeffrey here what you done to Clifford May.

Bower smiled through his mask of caked blood and lifted a table off the floor. In one motion he raised it high above his head and brought it down over his knee. The table disintegrated.

Goddamn, Jeff muttered.

Did you hear exactly what happened to Clifford May? Teddy said.

Got his back broken, Jeff said.

That's right, Teddy said. He called for another Jim Beam and a waitress with chopped, pink hair brought it to him. My associate Bower here snapped his spine clean in half.

Okay, Jeff said. I don't know nothing, all right? I just heard things.

Heard things, Teddy said.

Heard things, Jeff repeated.

Heard what kind of things? Teddy said.

I heard there were some pictures floating round, Jeff said. That's all and I don't even remember who it was that told me.

Oh, Jeffrey, Teddy said. You can do better than that.

Kill, kill, kill, kill, kill, Bower chanted amid the destruction he'd wrought.

That's all, Jeff said. Swear on my pop's grave, rest his soul.

Teddy ran his finger round the rim of his Jim Beam and shook his head. He said, You shouldn't bring your pop into this. Him and my old man were a dying breed. They had dignity and a sense of what was right and what was wrong.

Teddy, Jeff said. I know how you feel about that girl.

She's the only reason I got to be civilized these days, he said and called for Bower. Bower, he said, help Jeffrey here out of his seat.

Bower grabbed Jeff around the neck with one of his massive hands. He lifted him into the air, where Jeff hung and gagged like a trophy fish snagged from the water.

Please, Bill tried to say, but it came out as choking nonsense.

Teddy put down his Jim Beam and circled around behind Jeff as he dangled. He reached into his back pocket and slipped out a handful of photographs. For old times' sake, he said to Bower, give him some peace.

Bower tightened his grip and crushed Jeff's windpipe and neck. His head lolled forward and then Bower released him and let him crumple to the floor.

Teddy laid a wad of bills on the bar and walked out. It was really coming down outside and the streets and sidewalks and buildings were covered in a thick blanket of snow. Everything was blindingly white except for Teddy's dark green Jaguar parked out front.

Kill, Bower said, trying to cram his huge self into the passenger seat.

Teddy was behind the wheel and looking at the photographs. They were fuzzy and faded, but he could make out his girl lying on a bed, stepping out of a shower, splaying herself out for everyone to see.

I hear you, he said to Bower, to nobody. This here world ain't full of nothing but meanness anymore.

THE HATRED IN THEIR EYES, THE CRUELTY IN THEIR HEARTS

The neighbors are strange and prefer privacy over brotherhood. They keep to themselves. They sleep odd hours and complain to the police when I play my music loud. The only lights you ever see are in the basement. Connie thinks they have kinky sex down there. But I think it's something worse. A week ago the news said a boy got found in a ditch. Not a thing on him. You never know.

Last winter Connie took a peach pie over for the holidays. Little dark-eyed girl opened the door and said no thanks. Just no thanks. Really. Connie brought that damn pie back with her. Put it on the table in the kitchen and got the binoculars out of the cabinet, where we left them. She peered out our window and into theirs.

I don't understand it, she said, moving up on her tiptoes. You'd think I was giving them a bomb. She paused. Maybe I should give them a bomb, she said.

In the living room I was half-flipping through a magazine. I knew things were coming to a head. I'd seen them making love on their couch in the afternoon sun. I'd seen them kneel and kiss their child in his crib. Sooner or later they would come, and when they did it was going to be us or them.

MY BEAUTY IS SO HEAVY IT COULD CRUSH THE WHOLE OF THE WORLD

We took turns touching the warhead. Amanda was the braver of us two, setting the palm of her hand on the side and closing her eyes. I barely poked at it, expecting at any moment to jostle it just so that it would explode and destroy us and the silo and the house and the whole wide world above.

No need to worry, Commander Arsenic said. That motherfucker is a real piece of work.

Amanda and me had been down there all of two hours. We'd been digging up a space in the backyard for a pool. She didn't think we could do it ourselves, wanted to call on some professionals, but we didn't have the money for such things and I had a pretty big ego at the time. I figured I could trudge up enough dirt and then get in some concrete and we'd be lounging poolside with some margaritas before the week was over. Then I found the hatch and gave it a few knocks with the shovel.

What is that? Amanda said from the edge of the hole. She had a watered-down drink in hand. Is that some kind of spaceship?

No, I said. I think it's a silo. Government's got 'em hidden all over the country.

Pretty soon the hatch opened and Commander Arsenic and Private Blowtorch surfaced, hollow-eyed and emaciated. Truth be told, they looked four days past crazy. Congratulations, said Commander Arsenic. You found Silo Number Four-Thousand-Fifty-Niner.

Well, I said. Ain't that something?

It is something, Private Blowtorch said.

Permission to come aboard, I said.

You sure? Amanda said. Fear and drunkenness fogged her eyes.

I asked her when she'd been in a silo last.

Exactly, Commander Arsenic said. Come in and look around. We got drinks and snacks.

That was enough for Amanda, who didn't know how to turn anyone down who offered spirits. In fact, she took the lead and led us all into the silo, nearly running down the steel steps. A few feet in and we saw, in the distance, the tip of the missile Commander Arsenic and Private Blowtorch had nicknamed Hallelujah.

Hallelujah, Private Blowtorch explained, was commissioned in Nineteen-Eighty-Two.

She's been asleep ever since, Commander Arsenic said, pointing at a control panel with a blinking green light. She dreams of flying through the deep blue sky and separating in the troposphere.

Looks like she'd do some real damage, I said.

You don't know the half of it, Private Blowtorch said.

The two of them took us into the main control room, a good mile and a half underground. The cramped, circular room had everything you'd ever want. Coffee machines. Washer and dryer. An entire wall for TV viewing and a stereo stocked with every popular record up until Nineteen-Eighty-Two. Private Blowtorch pulled out a Merle Haggard live album and showed us how impressive the acoustics were.

Merle belted out a song about loving the US of A.

Holy shit, I said. That's impressive.

Damned right it's impressive, Commander Arsenic said. And that's just level four out of ten. You get that sucker up all the way and you'll be hurting.

It's a contingency, Private Blowtorch said and replaced the record with one full of children's songs. A syrupy voice sang for us a version of Old McDonald. If a war got going, Private Blowtorch said, you'd have to try and listen over all the explosions topside.

If a war got going, Amanda said dreamily.

We all can hope, Private Blowtorch said. He made a shaker full of martinis and handed me and Amanda and Commander Arsenic a glass. Maybe someday, he said.

Let's go take a look, Commander Arsenic said. Let's get you a glance at Hallelujah.

Amanda and me followed through another set of doors and into the actual silo itself. Machines whirred and the way lit by shaky fluorescent lights. Another set of stairs and we were climbing parallel to Hallelujah. On her side, in what appeared to be crazed, green spray paint, someone had scribbled the phrase TO ALL OF MINE ENEMIES, REAL AND IMAGINED, LET YE KNOW YR FATES.

Is that biblical? Amanda asked.

No, Commander Arsenic said. It's from the book Private Blowtorch is working on. Actually, he said, stopping on a stair and squinting his eyes, it's more of a tome. It passed beyond the realm of book a long, long time ago.

Up close Hallelujah was hypnotic in its grandeur. It felt as if you could stare at it for days and never really take it all in. I touched it first, but quickly pulled away. Amanda, as I've said, took more liberties.

She was born in Pittsburgh, Commander Arsenic said. A man named Dr. Leopold Jurgens completed her at nineteen hundred hours and she was loaded onto the back of a truck and smuggled under the cover of darkness.

All the way out here, Amanda said, stroking Hallelujah's side.

All the way out here, Commander Arsenic said.

Before too long Private Blowtorch joined us with another batch of martinis in hand. He took his turn touching the warhead and wept openly. As if pleading, he said, She's the most beautiful thing I've ever seen.

She's gorgeous, Amanda agreed.

A real piece of art, I said.

The finest thing America ever had to offer, Commander Arsenic said.

We took silent draws from our drinks.

Private Blowtorch removed a can of green spray paint from his pocket and shook it. He took in the missile like a hungry lover and depressed the button. When the deed was done a new phrase hung under the old one. This one read MY BEAUTY IS SO HEAVY IT COULD CRUSH THE WHOLE OF THE WORLD.

Perfect, Commander Arsenic said. Is that from a new chapter?

It is, Private Blowtorch said.

We admired Hallelujah and Private Blowtorch's art in silence for a good half hour. I shook myself from my trance and asked Amanda if we should go or stay.

Stay, she said. We have to stay.

You have to stay, Commander Arsenic said. We'll have more drinks.

So we stayed and had more drinks. Another round of martinis and then another. Commander Arsenic took the time to explain to us his philosophy of war and purification. It seemed, to him, that if mankind was to strive so hard to wipe itself out then it probably served to offer that they should be granted their wish.

If we want fire, he said between drinks, then we should have fire. If we want to reduce the world to ash and soot, then ash and soot we deserve.

Only in the burn do we find redemption, Private Blowtorch said.

It's simple math, Commander Arsenic said. The barbarism has a taste of its own and we are drunk in its steed.

I don't know if it was the liquor or the surroundings, but what Commander Arsenic was saying made a whole ton of sense. I could tell by looking at Amanda she thought so too. It's a real shame, I said, that she might never fire.

Private Blowtorch nodded somberly and wept again.

Forgive my associate, Commander Arsenic said. It's his greatest fear.

To imagine her sleeping forever, Private Blowtorch said. A wonderful creature set to hibernate from here to eternity. She deserves better, so much better.

She does, Amanda said. She had finished her martini and taken mine. Every bird deserves flight. Every fish a vast ocean.

Private Blowtorch had taken out a pad of paper and was furiously taking notes. Every fish a vast ocean, he repeated.

To imagine her sleeping in this hollow of earth, Amanda said, there couldn't be a worse thought.

Just think, Commander Arsenic said. You're walking home from the store. You're in Russia. You're in North Korea. You're in China. You're walking your rickshaw back from the farmer's market and a star descends from the sky. It's a perfect circle, a miniature sun floating so very gingerly down to the soil.

It's silent at first, Private Blowtorch said. A quiet, peaceful miracle.

It detonates like an angry god, Amanda said.

That's right, Commander Arsenic said.

A wall of flame and heat, I added.

The full and fiery fist of America, Private Blowtorch said.

We had another drink. We discussed our options.

You've made the point fairly well, Commander Arsenic said. We launch in an hour.

We had more drinks. We shook hands like happy heads of state.

If only we could see her fly, Amanda said.

That's part of the tragedy, Private Blowtorch said. He had his spray paint out again. We went with him to the missile and watched as he wrote THIS FAVOR OF DESTRUCTION I GIVE TO YOU, HAPPY IN HEART AND SOUL.

Another round of drinks. The world turned to soup in my eyes. Amanda traded martinis for Commander Arsenic's embrace. Private Blowtorch and I prepared the keys in the control panel.

Kiss me you cheap bastard, Amanda said to me, and I did.

At the agreed upon time Commander Arsenic and Private Blowtorch turned their respective keys. We sang America The Beautiful, but that turned to Old McDonald without so much as a thought. We were discussing the cows and their moos, the pigs and their oinks, the ducks and their quacks, as the belly of Hallelujah began to growl.

JENNIFER ANISTON COMES TO STAY AWHILE

Jennifer Aniston was waiting on the porch when I carried my shopping bags up the steps. I'd just come back from a trip to the Target, which'd involved a two and a half hour drive, both ways, the use of four different interstates, and an impressive amount of gas and time spent minding the lines. It had been worth it though as I'd finally found just the right shower caddy for my shower and had, for the first time in the two months since I'd moved into my new home, some hope in the matter of where to store my soap and shampoo and shaving cream and razor.

Are you Jennifer Aniston? I asked Jennifer Aniston while carrying my bags and shower caddy up the steps.

Cell phone pressed to her right ear, she said, Yes, hold on, and paused. The rays of the sun hit her just so that she glowed in the early-evening light. He's just arrived, she said into the phone, "I'll call you tomorrow, or the next day, or next week, or never. Okay," she said, pressing a button on her cell phone and sliding it into the pocket of her designer jeans. "Sorry about that. Hi, yes, I'm Jennifer Aniston. I've come to stay for awhile."

In most instances I would've balked and asked questions, but I was developing a new philosophy on life which included notions of positivity, adventure, and the power of saying yes. Things had been rough, terribly rough, and I was in need of a change. So I walked past her and unlocked the front door.

Jennifer Aniston seemed entirely comfortable in my home, which was still littered with boxes and unshelved books. She took a seat in one of my green chairs in the living room and told me how comfortable she found it. She was lying, of course, as my green chairs are notoriously uncomfortable and known to create dangerous pains in the back and lumbar region.

Would you like some water? I asked. Beer, milk, an old fashioned?

A martini, she said. Blue cheese crumbles.

Putting my bags to the side, along with my shower caddy, I opened my refrigerator and found it nearly empty. The contents included a rotten bag of salad mixings, half a stick of butter, a teapot of simple syrup, four bottles of Miller Lite, and a pot of leftover spaghetti.

You'll have to forgive me, I said, handing her one of the beers, I'm all out of blue cheese.

That's okay, she said and popped open the beer and took a sip. I used to drink these when I was a telemarketer. She wiped the foam from her perfect lips and let out a content sigh. I'd get off the phone, head to this bar called Taylor's, and knock back a couple before going home to my efficiency.

Probably seems like a lifetime ago, I said, thinking about how I'd seen her face on a tabloid in the checkout line at Target. The cover said she and her latest beau were on the outs because he wouldn't give her the child she so desperately wanted.

Four, she said. It seems like four lifetimes ago.

While she drank the beer I took my new shower caddy upstairs to my bathroom. The shower itself was a horror show, a mess of misplaced toiletries. My soap was a sudsy mess that teetered on the edge of one of the too-small ledges, the shampoo on the floor, my shaving cream and razor pushed exhaustedly in a corner. I took the shower caddy from the Target bag and hung it over the neck of the shower. It fit snugly into place and I put my toiletries on its shelves. I stepped back and smiled for the first time in weeks.

Would you look at that, Jennifer Aniston said. She had snuck into the bathroom with her beer and was admiring my new shower caddy.

Everything fits just right.

I said, This has been the bane of my existence. I haven't gotten a good night's sleep in I don't know how long.

Why didn't you just go to Target and get a shower caddy before? she asked. That seems like the logical solution.

Target's a two and a half hour drive, I said. It's in the next state over.

That's awful, Jennifer Aniston said between drinks of beer. My shower in my mansion is lined with secret compartments. All I have to do is say 'shampoo' and a compartment opens and there's my shampoo.

That must be perfect, I said.

No, she said, finishing that beer. It's awful. It's all awful.

After admiring my new shower caddy and shower system for a good, long time, Jennifer Aniston and I made dinner. I heated up

44

what was left of the spaghetti and she toasted some bread in the toaster oven. We had a few bites apiece before agreeing it was a terrible meal, and Jennifer Aniston was on her cell phone and calling up her personal chef from her mansion. He arrived in a tank-like vehicle with pictures of fine cuisine painted on the sides. When he jumped out of the tank-like vehicle's hatch he was carrying silver plates filled with fine cuisine. We sat on the porch, Jennifer Aniston and me, and ate the fine cuisine and drank Miller Lites.

I feel bad, she said.

Why would you ever feel bad? I said. The fine cuisine was just about the most perfect meal I'd ever eaten and I couldn't imagine ever being unhappy again with such fine cuisine.

I caved, she said. When I left my mansion this morning I swore to myself I'd give up these comforts. I was going to live like a human being again and appreciate the simpler things in life.

Nodding in agreement, I speared a piece of blackened cod with my fork and drug it through a smear of mango sauce.

My spaghetti's terrible.

Your spaghetti was fine, she lied. I'm just weak.

You're not weak, I said, though I wasn't sure if I believed what I was saying.

In the hours after dinner, as the sun set over the hills, we drove to the nearest gas station and bought more Miller Lites. We bought an ice chest too and two bags of ice and we shoved those Miller Lites into the ice chest and into the ice. They got cold and we drank more of them and watched the red rim of the dying sun cover the hills.

We were silent, Jennifer Aniston and me, and the world was silent too. Then her cell phone rang. She answered it with a grimace.

No, she said into the cell phone. It's not true, it's all garbage. We're pursuing different interests. That's all. She clicked the button on her cell phone and drained a full bottle of Miller Lite.

Leeches, she said.

Was that your agent? I said.

The press, she said. They want to know about William and me.

I'd seen this William, heard about him on the television. While unpacking my boxes the week before I'd seen a tabloid television show about stars and their personal lives and Jennifer Aniston and William, her beau, had been one of the leading stories.

Will William give Jennifer Aniston the baby she so desperately wants? the plastic-looking host asked us, the audience. Will he give her his seed and make her barren womb a lush forest of procreation?

When she'd asked this I instinctively looked up from my job and answered, I don't know, and had gone back to sorting my volumes of philosophy.

Will Jennifer Aniston ever find true happiness? the host asked. Will she ever climb out of her pit of despair and longing?

I don't know, I said again, thumbing through a dog-eared copy of *Das Capital*.

Look, the host said and I looked at the screen. It was filled with a video of Jennifer Aniston, elegant, radiant, strolling across a red carpet, William on her arm.

See her hidden longing, the host said.

I saw her hidden longing.

See how she burns, the host said.

I saw how she burned.

I looked at Jennifer Aniston, there on my porch, and saw how the burning had reduced to smoldering.

So, I said to her, what is the story with William and you?

You know, she said and then stopped. She considered the question. Her brow furrowed. She opened her mouth.

 I don't necessarily know what the story is.

Sure, I said. There were a lot of people in my life with whom I didn't know what our story was. Stories were always developing, changing. I couldn't, in that moment, put my finger on what my story was with anyone.

Say, I said. This is personal, but I should ask: do you want a baby?

Jennifer Aniston sat down the Miller Lite she'd been nursing. She wiped the beer's perspiration from her hands and worked her tongue in her cheeks. I could tell she was giving the question thought.

I don't know, she said. It seems like that's the question everyone wants to ask. That's the question they've been asking since I was with Brad Pitt. The question they've been asking for forever now.

To be honest, I said, it's a simple question.

In a way, she said, I guess it is a simple question. Either you want to have a baby or you don't. But in another way, it's the least simple question a human being can answer. I can understand the concept of having a baby, of expelling it from my womb and taking it home and raising it, feeding it, wiping drool from its blubbery lips, of teaching it my values and caring for it and shepherding it into its own life. But is understanding the concept enough?

No, I said, staring wide-eyed at Jennifer Aniston. No, I reckon it's not.

I don't think so either, she said. Because if you have that baby, if you expel it from your womb, there's not a whole lot of choice after that. The way I see it, you've been drafted into a whole different life, a whole other type of existence. You are stuck with that baby until you die or, god forbid, it dies. It's not like a shower caddy.

I perked up at the thought of my new shower caddy resting so perfectly around the neck of my shower.

 I don't reckon it is, I said. If I grow tired of my shower caddy, god forbid, I can just haul it off to the garbage.

That's right, Jennifer Aniston said. You can't very well haul a baby off to the garbage.

Jennifer Aniston and I stopped talking then and finished our Miller Lites. Once the sun had disappeared completely we went back into the house and made old fashioneds and got comfortable in my green chairs. She smiled and looked comfortable, but it was hard to believe what I was seeing was an accurate depiction of reality. Already my back was throbbing and my lumbar region knotting into angry fists.

What would you like to do? I said. I have a radio. I could turn on the television or put on a movie.

Let's watch a movie, Jennifer Aniston said. I'm in a real movie mood.

Good deal, I said and turned on the television. The way my television and DVD player were set up I had to first turn on the television and then press the appropriate buttons to switch to the channel where my DVDs played. It was a quick process, but as soon as I'd turned on the TV one of those tabloid shows popped up on the screen. They were showing video of Jennifer Aniston and I hurried and tried to make it disappear, but Jennifer Aniston, drinking an old fashioned in my green chair, told me to let it play.

Look, the plastic-looking host said to Jennifer Aniston and me. Look at the pain etched on her face. Look at how years of loneliness have carved ditches out of her Hollywood veneer.

I tried to stop myself, but I looked at the pain etched on Jennifer Aniston's face on the television. Then I looked at Jennifer Aniston, in my green chair, drinking an old fashioned, and looked at the pain etched on her face as if years of loneliness had carved ditches out of her Hollywood veneer.

The host said, Already reports have William paired with an up and coming, considerably younger, actress.

How about that? Jennifer Aniston said in my green chair.

I can turn it, I said. We don't have to watch this.

Let's watch, she said.

Look at the younger actress, the host said and I obeyed. It was a still photograph of a blonde-haired starlet emerging from the waves of an ocean, clad in a lime-green swimsuit and smiling the brightest smile I'd ever seen. Her skin was tanned bronze and her breasts large and impressive.

Notice her virility, the host said. Imagine her womb a thriving sea filled with life.

I noticed her virility and imagined her womb a thriving sea filled with life.

We've known each other a very short time, Jennifer Aniston said to me from my green chair. But will you be honest with me?

I swallowed hard and watched as the television showed more pictures of the young starlet at the beach. She and William were splashing water at one another and grinning like they'd be in love forever.

Yes, I said to Jennifer Aniston.

Good, she said, because I appreciate honesty. I appreciate honesty more than most anything else.

Me too, I said, not sure if I was lying.

All right, she said. Then be honest. When you look at that girl, that young starlet, do you see what the host asked you to see?

Virility? I asked. Her womb a thriving sea filled with life?

Yes, she said.

Yes, I said.

Jennifer Aniston narrowed her eyes and took a drink of her old fashioned.

So do I.

We watched the tabloid show for another four hours and drank another four old fashioneds apiece. We got drunk, Jennifer Aniston and me, and we didn't talk anymore. We were both fixated on watching that young starlet and William run along the edge of the water and kiss at the most appropriate times. I could tell the two of them loved one another and that theirs was a love destined to last. The plastic-looking host swooned on the soundstage and seemed to be falling in love with their love and her very existence seemed to improve as they blossomed into a healthy, mutually admiring and sufficient partnership before our very eyes.

Finally I had trouble keeping my eyes open and excused myself to my bedroom. I shucked my clothes into a pile by my hamper and retired to the bathroom. I turned on the hot water and stepped in under the spray. While my shower had never been anything to get excited about – the pressure was awful and the hot water heater had the potency of an old man – I had never been less happy with it in all the time I'd lived in that house. The way it spat lukewarm water at me served only to remind me how depressing my life had become. Even the presence of my new shower caddy and seeing how it held my soap and shampoo and shaving cream and razor did nothing for me.

I was just about to get out when Jennifer Aniston slipped open the shower curtain and joined me under the spray. She was nude and I could see how years with a Hollywood personal trainer had helped to sculpt a physique that most women would murder for. When she moved it was with an elegance I'd never witnessed, and when she kissed me it was a kiss unlike any I'd ever received.

We started to make love in the shower but the loss of heat was too great to finish, so we went into my bedroom and finished on top of the comforter. Jennifer Aniston lay below me and stroked my hair and told me she'd finally found home. She was ready to give it all up, the award shows, the movie sets, the interviews, the magazine spreads, the fundraisers and pressers, the whole nine yards. She said all she needed was me and a child of our own.

Please, she said. Give me what I've always wanted.

It was no time at all before I was grunting and wheezing. I stroked her hair back and thought of my own shower with hidden compartments and on-demand shampoo. I thought of summoning a chef and seeing his tank-like vehicle climbing the hills and how he'd emerge with silver trays of fine cuisine. I thought of seeing myself on the tabloid covers as I stood in line at a nearby Target, my shopping cart filled to the brim with the most expensive shower caddies a man could buy.

I almost let go and gave Jennifer Aniston her wish. Almost. But as I neared that precipice, as she urged me to go on, a new thought supplanted the others. This was clearer, more vivid, so strong in fact that it moved me to tears. Jennifer Aniston saw the tears and stroked my hair and nodded as if to reassure.

It's going to be all right, she said, and I said yes, it would be.

It's going to be a beautiful baby, she said, and I said yes, the most beautiful baby.

In my mind though I was already sitting in a chair on a beach, sipping a cool drink, the Target-cart full of shower caddies at my side, a whole world of cameramen focused on my every move, my love, my one true love, bounding out of the ocean, her lime-green swimsuit bursting at the seams, a whole world of life and light whispering yes, yes, forever and ever.

HABIT YOURSELF TO THE DAZZLE OF THE LIGHT

When Valerie met her husband Rich in The Fog it was sometimes distracting how his body would be surrounded by a golden aura. She had tried to ignore it at first, imagined it was some heavenly luminescence, but she'd never been successful at disregarding it completely. Its nagging existence bothered her so much she could hardly focus on their bouts of marathon virtual lovemaking set in exotic and impressive locales. To try and remedy the problem, she contacted the operating company FogCo and put in a request for tech support.

No worries, a reply appeared instantly. Developers have already included a halo fix into the upcoming software upgrade Fog 4.0.

Valerie knew the new operating system was due out in three days, a virtual eternity in Fog-Time. After all, when plugged into the virtual-existence simulator time, as she had known it in pre-Singularity days, came to a practical standstill. She and Rich could dance their way around the world and back, travel through the artificial stars and galaxies, live entire lives and conquer dreams and empires, in what roughly amounted to a half hour in real existence.

To wait another three days for a fix to her problem was akin to receiving a life sentence in Purgatory.

What's the matter? Rich asked, thrusting away at her. They were on an paradisiacal island. Breathtakingly beautiful birds were soaring above them and serenading them with an auto-tuned croon. You seem distracted, he said.

It's nothing, she said. She was filled with complete physical pleasure, which had become her natural state of being. But she wasn't able to fully focus on the pleasure or appreciate the pleasure because of the glow emanating from Rich's skin. Instead, she was staring at the sky and how the hologram twinkled like stars at a distance.

Rich pulled away from her with his upper body while his lower half continued its thrusting in perfectly-timed piston-like undulations. He asked her, Is it the glow again?

With a sigh she relented. Yes, she said. It's the glow.

Would you like me to stop?

No, she said. Yes. Either way.

A few seconds later Rich yielded and sat beside her. Despite being eighty years old he appeared as he had when he was twenty-six, when they'd first met at a dinner party. His hair was expertly parted and his body statuesque. He gazed off at the birds and the digitized volcano that loomed over them. I'm sorry about the glow, he said after a moment.

It's fine, she said and raised herself up onto her elbow. Doesn't it bother you?

No, he said matter-of-factly.

Do you see it?

Sometimes, he said and picked a leaf of grass from the dirt. He smelled it, bringing a smile to his face before he let it go and watched it swim away on the breeze. I've learned to ignore the glitches, he said.

What glitches?

Oh, he said, the small ones. The way the air sizzles before we change locations. How nothing smells quite right. Like plastic.

I can handle the plastic smell, Valerie said.

Your eyes sparkle, Rich said. Particularly when I apply one of the older skins.

Valerie cocked her head. Somewhere a lone bird was singing the same tune its family was crooning but the program had glitched and it sounded less like a melody than a printer growling out a stretch of paper. Richard, Valerie said, are you applying a skin to me right now?

Without shame Richard admitted he was.

What skin?

Female Model Subset 42 A, he said.

With a thought Valerie applied Female Model Subset 42 A and Rich transformed instantly into an impossibly buxom model clad in a yellow string bikini. Her long and immaculate hair hung down over her heaving breasts and tickled the bed of grass.

I can't believe you, Valerie said. I cannot believe you.

What? he said, his gorgeous blue eyes sparkling unnaturally.

We agreed that we wouldn't use skins anymore.

When?

I don't know, Valerie said. It's gotten hard keeping track of time. Awhile back. We agreed.

I didn't agree to that, Rich said.

A bell sound played and Valerie's visual display received another message from FogCo. No worries, it said again, Developers have already included a halo fix into the upcoming software upgrade Fog 4.0.

Disable, Valerie thought and the message disappeared.

Let's go to Rome, Rich said. Let's screw on the steps of Saint Peter's. Or load one of the history applications.

I'm tired, Valerie said. I can't believe how tired I am. She crawled her eyes down the bikini model's body. Default, she thought and the bikini model disappeared and was replaced by Rich as he had been when they'd first entered The Fog. He was feeble, spotted and covered in smatters of black, gray, and white hair. His flesh hung loosely in folds and his face was wrinkled and pathetic. Past Richard, Valerie panicked and thought. Past Richard. Soon he was back to his idealized self, the glow returned and blazing as if in accusation.

Use a revitalization app, Rich said. Boost up and we'll go back to The Renaissance and fuck in DaVinci's studio. We could do it in Cleopatra's bedchamber or among the Hanging Gardens of Babylon.

I'm logging off, Valerie said.

Rich recoiled in horror. What?

I'll be back, she said and then thought, Log off. A notice appeared: Are you sure? I'm sure, Valerie thought and immediately the air crackled with violence and her vision was replaced with a thick and milky sleep from which she had to emerge. She fought her way through and when her eyes opened, with much protest, she found she was sitting in the living room of the their house. It was dark, the room filled with shadows. Rich, in his undershirt and trousers, sat on the nearby loveseat, his eyes closed and mouth hanging open.

Valerie worked the life back into her limbs before crossing the distance between them and gently touching his chin to close his mouth. She felt his skin and marveled at how different it was outside The Fog.

Softer.

Rougher.

She stood looking at him until a light flashed from outside. It lit up the room momentarily before another followed. Valerie knew it was a Spark Ad, one of the countless pop-ups that were everywhere now. She went to the window and gazed outside at the empty streets and all of the surrounding houses, dark and seemingly abandoned. The world looked deserted except for the sad-sack moon hanging overhead among a sky devoid of stars. The air below sizzled with budding advertisements – smell apps, taste apps, skin apps, travel apps, emotion apps and inspiration apps – that appeared and disappeared as random as neon ghosts. She searched among their clutter for any sign of life before calling up her clock app. An invisible nanobot, one of the infinite of which populated the air like so much pollen, projected the time and date. Three days, Valerie told herself, returning to the couch to wait.

HELP

B and M were busily watching television and eating their prepared dinners when M suffered a pain in her stomach so great she doubled over and fell to the floor. The program B and M were watching on their television was a game show called What Happens Next? where viewers were invited to watch a short video and, once the video had stopped, shout out-loud what they thought would happen next. At the time of M's excruciating pain a video was playing of a man running full-speed into a brick wall. As M fell to the floor the video stopped with the man merely inches from the wall and in full-stride.

He's going to hit that damn wall, B yelled at the television screen.

My stomach hurts bad, M said and writhed on the ground.

Hold on, B told M. I want to see what happens next.

The video of the man running full-bore at the brick wall unpaused and the man, just as B had predicted, ran right smack-dab into the wall. The impact sent him sprawling into a moaning, crying heap on the ground.

It hurts so bad, M said to B.

I bet it does, B said. He ran right into that wall.

No, M said. I'm talking about my stomach.

B stood up from the couch he was sharing with M and sat his prepared dinner on the coffee table in front of them. He looked at M and watched her writhe on the ground in pain. Do you think it has anything to do with that big bump of yours? he asked her.

I don't know, M said. Maybe. That would explain a lot of things.

It sure would, B said. You've had that bump for a while now.

M bit her lip. Too long, she said.

B did the only thing he could think of doing. He ran into the kitchen and hit the button marked HELP that was placed on the wall next to the box where they kept their prepared meals. A red light above the button marked HELP flashed and B ran back to M, still on the floor.

I hit the HELP button, he said.

Good, M said. It's only getting worse.

The pain or the bump? B said.

The pain, M said. I don't know if the bump's getting worse.

B leaned and observed M's bump. From what he could tell the bump had not grown since the pain had started. Looks okay to me, he said to M.

Good, M said. The last thing I need is to hurt and have that bump get worse.

In twenty minutes time help had yet to arrive, so B helped M back up onto the couch. He got his prepared dinner and her prepared dinner and the two of them sat on the couch and watched more What Happens Next? on the television. A woman on the show was staring inquisitively at a hammer in her hand.

When the video paused B asked M what she thought would happen.

I don't know, M said. All I can do is sit here and hurt.

I thin she's going to hit herself, B said. That's what's getting ready to happen.

Okay, M said. I feel like something's moving.

Is it the pain? B said. Or is it the bump?

I don't know, M said. I'm not a doctor.

B said, I know you're not a doctor.

There was a knock at the door. B got up, upset about the way M had talked to him, and opened the door and let the help in. The help consisted of an old man wearing a tie and a white doctor's coat and a robot carrier unit that rolled around on six wheels. The old man and the robot carrier unit approached M on the couch.

What seems to be the problem? the old man asked M.

I got this pain in my stomach, she said.

Uh huh, the old man said.

Beep, the robot carrier unit said.

Let me ask you a question, the old man said. Have you had a bump for a while now?

A few months, M said. I don't know how long.

Has it gotten bigger and bigger? the old man said.

Yeah, M said. Can't you see it?

I can, the old man said.

Beep, the robot carrier said.

Tell you what, the old man said. Let's get these pants off, what do you say?

Pants? M said.

It's best to do what he says, B said. I think he's a doctor.

I am a doctor, the old man assured them.

Okay, M said, unbuttoning her pants with great difficulty.

The old man got into position on the floor and the robot carrier until followed him. It beeped and whirred as he manipulated M. B stood off to the side, eating his prepared meal. Thirty minutes later and the old man was pulling a wriggling, goo-covered person out of M. B and M watched the process in utter shock.

Is that a little person? B asked.

I think so, M said.

It was inside you? B said.

I think so, M said. I think it was inside me.

Oh god, B said.

It's a perfectly normal procedure, the old man said while wiping the person off with his handkerchief. As old as time itself, he said.

Beep, the robot carrier unit said. Beep beep.

You'll find, the old man said, that the bump will go away on its own.

Did you hear that? M said to B, panting. He said the bump's going to go away on its own.

Sure thing, the old man said. He lowered the person to the level of the robot carrier unit. A shelf in the unit's chest popped out and the old man placed the person snugly onto it. When the shelf rescinded B and M looked at the person through a transparent window in the unit's chest.

Who is that person? B said.

I don't know, M said. I don't know him.

No you don't, the old man said. Take care of yourselves now, he said, leaving the apartment with the robot carrier unit and person in tow.

Man alive, B said. I'm glad about that bump.

Me too, M said.

You've been worried about that bump for a while now, B said.

Too long, M said. Say, what happened with that girl and the hammer?

The girl with the hammer? B said. The one who was looking at the hammer on the TV? I don't know.

Damn it, M said. I really wanted to know how that turned out.

ON THE EMPIRE CITY

The afternoon before, on the beach, Tybee Island, a group of rebel flag bathing suits bathing before us. My friends all scholars. PhDs ladled upon PhDs. Comparative Literature. British Literature. Metaphysics and Existentialism. A gallon of cocktails at our feet and our feet buried deep in the hot sand.

Why dread a trip to New York City? my colleague asked. Is it not the Mecca of Western Culture? Is it not the center of all that is good and known?

I bristled. Anyone who has spent more than an afternoon in the presence of my brilliance knows my thoughts on the Empire City. Rotted with blight. Saturated to the gills. Self-involved and brutish. A perfect metaphor for the lackings of The Dream, a village of skeletons climbing over one another.

Professor Bolanski, I answered. Your Mecca is another man's compost pile. Call on me in two days time and you will find a wounded and sorrowful man.

But Professor Bullet, they said. A man of renowned culture and sensibilities such as yourself no doubt has affection for The Big Apple.

Bah, I said and downed the last of my cocktail. A grit of sand and earth dripped between my teeth and I swallowed hard. Who needs culture? I said. Who needs sensibilities?

Of course they knew I was being facetious. I had published several volumes about culture and many more about sensibilities. My name was well known among the initiated.

To Professor Bullet, one of my colleagues toasted. May his journey north be full of splendor.

Hungover and dissatisfied, I climbed aboard a commuter train bound and determined for New York City. I would have avoided such a trip at any cost had a close and dear friend of mine not been in need. He had called a few days before and informed me as to his plan to drink himself into a stupor and then jump off the Williamsburg Bridge.

Bullet, he slurred over the line, I've seen too much. This goddamned city has hardened my heart to limestone. I've witnessed the downfall of man. I'm capable of so much testimony as to the weight of human hardship.

I should have known such a moment was coming. He was a correspondent for *Newsweek* and spoke at length about the American Consciousness. At first it was features about home ownership. First-generation college graduates. Then mothers who had weened themselves off food stamps. Finally the burden of postmodern, post-colonial, globalist guilt. He guided photographers into dying and dead communities and hung his byline over the portrait of rusted farmhouses and foreclosed single-family ranch homes. The week before, outside of a cathedral, he'd tried to interview a seventy-year-old woman who'd hurled herself off the roof and onto the waiting spikes of the gate below.

The jig is up, he'd said with certitude.

Was there ever a jig? I asked. I was half-drunk off a bottle of gin. I had few scruples. I asked for details about the seventy year old woman. Did she hit square? I had asked. Did she leave a note? I had asked.

There never was a jig, he cried into the receiver. The American Experiment is over. It's failed worse than a middle-schooler's tinkerings. Come and witness me sour my liver, he said. Come and watch me pickle.

He was a good man, my friend who worked for *Newsweek*, and I had no choice. In graduate school he held my head many a night. He had fixed more than a few breakfasts. He had counseled me when I felt the world a dark and lonely place. Now I recognized him as a fellow traveler down the electrocuting highway of nihilistic indifference.

Stay your hand, I begged him. Have a drink to settle and then back away from the bottle. Maybe two drinks, but no more. I will assist you, I said. I will help the same way you helped me when I was just a sexually frustrated teaching assistant.

The train arrived on time, thank god. I was standing among a crowd of tank-topped strangers who whistled at the young women walking in and out of the Planned Parenthood across the street. A few threw handfuls of peanuts and pulled down their swim trunks and exposed themselves. Savannah was a rough town full of cretins. Villains and cowards. To frequent a bar there was to play with your life. When the engine rounded the bend I was about to assert myself and ask for some sort of décor, but luckily the conductor rolled to a well-timed rescue.

Why not fly? you might ask. Why shouldn't we all fly? Well, perhaps some of us had boarded a flight ten years before and drank one too many cups of overpriced champagne and engaged a voluptuous flight attendant in a discussion as to the merits of physics. Perhaps some of us used words like sudden loss of altitude and statistical certainty. Or perhaps it was the persistent chanting of phrases like inevitable mechanical failure. Perhaps it was some combination or all of these things. Perhaps it was fate. Perhaps it was a rare miscalculation that forced some of us aboard a sixteen-hour ride of nationally subsided travel.

Whatever led to the situation led to the situation. I sat in Seat 57 and immediately pulled from my flask. Being a man of superior faculties I had planned ahead and filled it with a splash of Black Label. It flooded my mouth and I gazed across the aisle. A man in a red Hawaiian shirt had similarly prepared. He was pulling cans of Coors Light from a backpack huddled in the neighboring seat.

Road soady? he offered.

Nip of brown? I offered right back.

We traded spirits. We both sunk into our respective areas and clambered down. The next six hours I tried to ply my trade over a stack of dimestore pulp novels. I had a theory at the time that lowbrow entertainments were better windows into the layman's soul that any census, study, or fact-finding jaunt could ever hope to be. They were filled with bared breasts and slick-oiled guns. Promiscuous trysts. Moonshine stills and drug-runners. I jotted down notes on a clean sheet of my legal pad and considered the possibilities. I was circling in the intellectual air over something large, something true.

Excuse me, came a voice a from behind.

I turned and found a woman wearing a blouse covered in happy-looking skulls, the kind of shirt one found on the rack nearer to Halloween. It was May though and the gesture a clumsy one.

Yes, my dear, I said.

I noticed you had a flask, she said in the weakest of voices.

I do, I said.

Care to share? she asked sheepishly.

Certainly, I said and handed her my flask. She screwed open the cap and downed a healthy chug. Have another, I said. She looked tired and worn past the point of pride. I figured her to be someone who had loved and lost. She could've fit right into one of my pulps. She could've been the prom queen turned reject, the happy little toy who'd lost a few screws or coat of paint and found herself travelling cheaply up the coast.

Why thank you, she said and had another drink. You're a gentleman.

Guilty, I said and took back my flask. The next glug warmed me from toe to ear. The rocking of the car was starting to ease me into a kind sleep. I grabbed my pillow and fitted it behind my weary head. Say, I said, looking at the woman again and the man she was sitting next to. He had an unruly white beard dripped through with tobacco juice. Care to join me? I asked her.

Why, it was like she was fired out of gun and into my seat. She settled in and sighed happily. A true gentleman, she said.

Certainly, I said and waded into a gentle sleep.

The dreams I had were easy ones. Childhood remembrances. Listening to my father lecture on the ethics of experimentation. Watching he and mother and my brother Lee push off on their skiff and into the waiting bay. An umbrella opening in a spitting summer storm.

The last vision woke me and I found my lap invaded by the woman's hand. Her fist was tucked into the waistband of my slacks.

Her face was hungry and glowing. Five dollars, she said mid-pump. I know you're close, she said, fish out your wallet and I'll make sure you get all the way.

I nearly screamed. Prostitution. On a train. Such poor form.

Ma'am, I said, reaching for my belt and button. You have misjudged me. You have severely misread this situation.

She reached out with a fistful of claws and cut my face. A curtain of blood rushed over my eyes and I lashed out and pushed her into the aisle. Her skull-covered blouse came loose and her breasts flopped out like twin loaves of meat dropped haphazardly onto a dirty picnic table. Bastard, she yelled and clutched her blouse closed. Bastard, bastard, bastard.

Bullet, I said and closed my belt buckle. Professor Bullet at that.

My would-be prostitute didn't even wait for the next stop to abandon ship. She ran to the area that connects coach to dining and forced open the sliding door, disappearing with a great whoosh.

It was enough for me to hit my flask again and try and calm my wounded nerves. The gall of some people, I thought. The nerve it takes to seek advantage over a fellow traveler, a man of letters nonetheless.

Satisfied the threat had been neutralized, I returned to my slumber and remained there until morning. The first hint of light stroked my face and I awoke to a moving landscape unlike any other. There were farmlands, fields of wheat and soy. The trees seemingly cooperated and framed the wonderful scene. It was enough to stroke a man to the side of destiny and goodness. It was enough to make me question all the pessimistic dogma I'd been chasing the better part of my squalored existence.

I was considering this possibility, the chance I had misjudged the nature of our very reality, when I spied the first carcass. Then another. Then another. Dozens upon dozens. Heifers and bulls bloated along the track. Farmers and hands holding smoking shotguns. The foreground sizzling with cooking meat.

Moo, said the man across from me who had smuggled the beer aboard. Moooooooooooooo, he said and cackled.

The train stopped and the stench swarmed through the car. The main door opened and a new group of weary travellers boarded. There were desperate-looking, drunk and hungry. One, a boy of maybe thirteen jumped the step and hurried into the seat next to mine.

Howdy, he said and crossed his legs in a feminine way.

Howdy, I said back.

I stabbed a man this morning, he said. He searched my face to see what I made of that. He couldn't have grown a beard if he was held hostage. Out of his pocket he pulled a pack of gum and tossed three sticks into his mouth. He was my sister's boyfriend, he said. He asked too many questions.

How many are too many? I asked.

You're halfway there, he said.

Being a man of above-average intelligence I picked up on his warning. I returned to my pulp novels and studied the simple language of barbarian scribes. A woman was tossed on a bed and offered to a debt-holding dealer. She called the name of her father and then the priest who'd presided over her confirmation.

You ever wonder about things? the murderer next to me asked.

I knew better than to answer. I'd used up my one question and wasn't about to tempt fate. Earlier I'd noticed the outline of a deboning knife in the pocket of his blue jeans. Instead I returned to my sentences and watched out of the corner of my eye as he picked the piping of his sneakers.

I wonder about things a lot, he said. I wonder what causes savagery. About what leads to hatefulness. I wonder why somebody would do the things I do. I wonder about fate and if maybe the universe is one giant instrument. Maybe we don't know how to play it. Maybe God's the only one and maybe he's a real sonuvabitch. Maybe the strings to that instrument are our genetic code. Maybe he's playing a real mean-ass symphony whenever I dig in with my blade.

The words I read clumped together in an ink-colored cloud. He became she and she became he. I reread the same line over and over.

The bagman twirled his gun and fired a round into the floor.
The bagman twirled his gun and fired a round into the floor.
The bagman twirled his gun and fired a round into the floor.

It was too much. I looked out my window and half-expected to see more carnage. Instead a turn approaching. I saw the skeleton of the tracks curving like disease. I thought my friend was wrong. New York wasn't the center. It wasn't the Mecca. It was the beating, thrumming heart. We were hustling down a collapsed vein, we oxygen-thin cells.

I wondered if I was cancer.

I wondered if I was a crink in the genetic code.

At the next stop I stood at the station among the smokers. The boy with the deboning knife watched me intently from a window on the train. One of the men from earlier exposed himself again to a passing woman. She stopped, regarded him, studied him, and continued.

I was close, he said.

We were two hours outside New York. The air was changing. There was threat in the molecules. Misunderstanding and short nerves. In the distance the bruise that was the city. I asked the boy with the deboning knife if he had ever been before.

You bet, he said. I left a trail too.

And this time? I followed.

They'll never forget my name.

I read the same sentence again. The bagman twirled his gun and fired a round into the floor. I got the boy with the deboning knife's attention and had him read it. He approved. I approved. The words a cloud of ink again. The air cruel.

At Penn Station we deboarded and stood in the swirling crowd. The times changed on the board and I was forgotten. The boy with the deboning knife unsheathed his weapon and swam into the gathering with hungry intentions. I grabbed the nearest payphone and called my friend. He didn't answer so I called the offices of *Newsweek*. They didn't answer either.

I stood on the platform and closed my eyes. It was all I could do. I closed my eyes and listened to the hum of the people surrounding me. Who knows what I was waiting for? Perhaps a nudge? Perhaps a quick call from my friend or his begrieved cohorts at *Newsweek*? Perhaps the gasp and screams my associate with the deboning knife would soon elicit? Or, perhaps, there on the pulsing aorta of America, I was waiting to be played. For my string to be acted upon. For a song to be plucked out of me, like a good and obedient instrument should.

MR. WIMBLEDON

Rains here every afternoon. Two-thirty. You could set your watch by it. You'll be looking out the window, admiring the way the sun licks the hydrangeas across the street, and then all of a sudden it's Noah's Flood out there. And here's the thing: the dirt holds the water like a bowl. Doesn't even soak into the soil. You're just watching and wondering where the hell all that water goes.

I like to ask Sue what she thinks sometimes. She doesn't talk much but when she speaks you know she means it. Hon, I say to her, what do you make of this rain situation?

She shrugs most of the time. After awhile you start to realize there are different kinds of shrugs. I don't know shrugs, for sure, but shrugs that say yeah or nay or how in the hell am I supposed to know?

Sue's got a shrug that tells me we ought to go out for dinner, if you can believe it.

As a matter of survival we moved down to South Carolina. We were having ourselves a hell of a time up in Ohio before we called it quits. Sue had an ex there who swung by every day while I was at work. I had an ex who swung by whenever Sue was at work. I tell you, we were more or less running a hotel.

I stand at the window in the front room and wait for the deluge. There's a fella walking his big yellow dog out there. He's wearing white shorts, white shoes, white shirt. I think he plays tennis sometimes at the high school. He moved down here the week before last and if I heard him right he's from Pennsylvania.

My memory's not what it used to be because of the booze.

Anyway, he hasn't learned the schedule. He's out there with that big yellow dog, the one that gets loose sometimes and tears up the hydrangeas and every other matter of planted flower or bush in the neighborhood, and he's sunning himself in the afternoon glow. Then it just pours. Like the hammer of god.

Those white shorts?

His white shoes?

That white shirt?

They're practically nothing after a half second in the storm.

Sue, I say. You wouldn't believe this shit.

She shrugs a shrug that means she probably wouldn't believe this shit.

The new neighbor, Mr. Wimbledon? Just got caught in it.

She shrugs.

Sue, I say.

She shrugs again.

Sue, I wish you wouldn't be like that about our neighbor.

Another.

Sue, I'm only a man. I've still got my pride.

Mr. Wimbledon takes off down the street with the yellow dog in tow. He rounds the bend and heads off in the direction of the courts. Maybe he's planning on getting a few sets in. How am I supposed to know?

I pace around the house thinking about what it used to be like. How I'd come home for lunch and find Sue and her ex in compromising positions. They liked the couch. Hell, they liked the floor just as much. I'd open the door and yell, I'm home, just to give them a chance to get decent. Not that they took it.

Sue, I say, how could you have done all that? With your ex? The couch? The floor?

She shrugs and it's as if she's saying, There are different kinds of love. At least that's what I think she means. It's what she always used to say before she told me she wouldn't say it no more.

There's no sense in trying to get anything else out of her. She's made up her mind in these matters. She's only got so many words and none of them are going to be used digging up the past. She even said that one time.

I didn't have any choice but to sit there and nod.

In no time the storm dies and the sun takes its rightful place. The water that'd stood on the dirt sucks on down to the core of the Earth or wherever the hell it goes. Looking out there, you could almost forget it ever rained at all.

A MONUMENT FOR THE DEAD

There was a decision to build a memorial to victims of war. The President, newly elected, was soft of heart and tired of warfare and its ravages being accepted by the general public. In a speech on the television he said the time had come for the consequences to be seen by one and all. Too many times, he said, the battlefields of old had been cleared and cleaned and disinfected and, as a result, our constant appetite for destruction and death had gone unencumbered.

The plans were put into motion at once. For maximum effect and visibility The President and his blue-ribbon team of advisors chose Times Square as the location for the site of the new monument and got work choosing a method of remembrance.

An artist from NYU suggested a reflection pool where visitors could peer into the water and see themselves as potential casualties of future wars. A design team based in Nacogdoches presented a plan to litter the area with numerous headstones inscribed with the names of all of the major skirmishes of modern times. Both were considered and put to public vote, but ultimately the decision was made to fill the square with made-to-scale fake bodies. The woman responsible for this plan said it would go the furthest in terms of ultimately presenting an accurate portrayal of the cost of war.

The next step was to decide what size the fake bodies would be and it was argued, by the liberal side of the aisle, that all manner of sizes and ages and sexes and nationalities be represented. In the beginning this was fought by the conservative contingent, which said it would be more financially prudent to simply produce a single mold for the bodies. The President though, invigorated by the momentum of his idea, brokered a deal between the factions and it was decided that three molds would be produced – an adult-sized male, an adult sized-female, and a child-sized doll. The Sexuality Movement, however, fought this decision as being far too representative of heteronormative values and were accommodated following a lengthy and tumultuous filibuster. Finally, after three years of legal battles, campaigns, and elections, it was determined that there would be two molds produced by the government, this time an androgynous adult-sized figure and that of a child.

Following the resolution the country's manufacturing went into full swing and produced the first wave of bodies. They were dyed stark white in an effort not to denote any particular race and stacked in warehouses and shipped to New York City. Some workers went as far as to draw faces on the bodies and some dressed them in castoff clothes and put notes in their pockets. The economy skyrocketed and people found themselves flush with earnings and bought new cars and clothes and jewelry and televisions and homes. Young and old, educated and uneducated, black and white, everyone prospered and saw profit. The President was reelected in a landslide and promised to continue his policy of building toward a memorial for victims of war.

A controversy arose though over how many of these bodies should be manufactured. The President charged his blue-ribbon team of advisors to determine exactly how many people should be represented. The first figure was one million. People respect the sum one million, an advisor explained. At that point, however, more than one million bodies had been manufactured and there were no signs of the production slowing. Another advisor suggested they try for one billion, another round number, but The President had other plans.

I want to know exactly how many people have died from the scourge of war, he said over lunch one day. Every last one.

What followed was a three-month, around the clock, investigation and tabulation. Experts were flown in from the major mathematics and history departments around the country. Scholars and academics argued nonstop for a hundred days, taking breaks only to refresh their anger and fetch books from the provided library. Some of them, the ones with degrees or interest in philosophy, suggested that war was merely a state of mind and had never technically killed anyone or anything.

Your answer, one professor told The President, is exactly zero bodies. No body should ever be produced, or should have ever been produced, because war is not something that has ever existed.

The President sat and thought over what the professor had said. Those at the meeting expressed later that they could see the very gears of The President's brain milling over such a concept. The President was an intellectual, after all, and he thought over every suggestion ever offered him. Then, in a quick and unexpected moment, The President leapt from his chair, crawled across the table dividing him and the professor, and sunk his teeth into his neck. Blood from the professor's neck rolled out over The President's lips and The President let him go after his point was made. The professor clamped his hand over the wound and scurried out of the meeting.

So, The President said. The matter at hand.

The agreed upon number of bodies was five billion. The factories stepped up their schedules and the goal was reached within the year. Fleets of flatbed trucks rolled into Times Square and teams of workers chucked the adult and child-sized bodies into a pile. The pile grew quickly and spread through the adjoining streets. Even when piled on top of one another the five billion bodies filled the whole of New York City and residents of the boroughs were forced out by martial law. As they left the city they were replaced, in their homes and businesses, by the blank bodies representing the dead.

When The President held the ceremony marking the opening of the new monument there were celebrations around the country. It was considered the new quintessential American landmark. Families came from far and wide to see the newly transformed New York City. They bought T-shirts from vendors in the streets and took pictures of themselves among the bodies. The President was conflicted. While his dream had been realized and his approval numbers had soared, he was not yet pleased. The monument had the air of accomplishment to it, the feeling that it was a great achievement instead of a somber place of reflection. Wars continued around the world and the country even faced its own escalating conflict that showed no signs of abating.

What do we do about this? The President asked, haggard from several nights' worth of insomnia. How do we charge this area with its required grisly tone?

The blue-ribbon team of advisors considered the question. The answer came to the junior member of his staff in his dreams. The young man had been working so hard on the proposition it had seeped into his unconscious mind. When he sat down to eat and carved into expensive steaks, all he could see were the white forms of the bodies. When he made the opening incision in his baked potato, the resulting action was more akin to a ribcage bursting forth with viscera and gore. In his dreams he began to see fields of dead, mountains of the massacred. He saw formless persons crawling among the carnage, their voices little more than sighs. Even in his REM cycle the young man could smell the stench of decay and the rotting of flesh. Packs of flies the size of migrating birds swarmed the sky and the sound was like an army of motors singing into the night.

Mr. President, he said. This experiment will never work unless we are to fully realize the scorn of war. We need meat and we need flesh. Blood and bile and bleached bones sinking into the soil.

The President, ever one to see merit in a good idea, put a plan into place. The country's slaughterhouses and blood banks donated their unusable fluids to the government. Fields of cattle were butchered and dumped over the monument. Forty tons worth of filth and feces transported via tanker trucks and sprayed upon the area. Entire cemeteries emptied and moved to New York Island, the bones and bits of decomposed matter sprinkled randomly. The effort revitalized an economy already feeling the sting of the monument's completion. The unemployed and underemployed were taken to the site of the monument and worked in shifts to properly coat every wall and floor and body with the mixture.

On the final day The President boarded a boat in the harbor and brought with him the entirety of his cabinet and the young man. When the sun set vapors rose off the island as if it were a massive pool of gasoline. Hordes of birds and flies flew across the sky and blacked out the sun for miles around. The sound was like the young man's dream, as if some massive engine had been started and would never stop again.

LIKE THE OLD DAYS

Everything changed for Judy and me when the baby came along. Suddenly it was the baby this, the baby that. Judy got so worried about Rich, our son, that she couldn't sleep. She'd sit there in his room and watch him, making sure he never stopped breathing. It got to be that we never talked about anything but the baby, never went anywhere without the baby, never did anything that didn't have the baby right square in the middle of it.

That went on for years. Rich got older, but Judy never backed off. She was always layering on the clothes in the winter, keeping him inside during the summer. Rich got to the point where he was soft and scared all the time. You're babying him, I said to Judy. You're going to get him where he's afraid of his own shadow.

You don't understand the first thing about it, she said. What would you know anyway? You spend half your life drunk anymore.

She had a point. Since Rich came along there wasn't anything else to do. After work I went out and had beers and smoked a few with my buddies and then came home and drank some more there. By the time I came in she'd have Rich in bed and be sitting there at the kitchen table, staring at the wall. Guess you're drunk again, she'd say.

I'd say, Guilty as charged.

We went two years there where we were never together.
That's a problem. A man and his wife have to be alone sometime.
Everybody knows that.

When Rich was seven I took a look at him and then at Judy.
The boy needs friends, I said.

He's got friends, Judy said. You have friends, don't you
sweetheart?

Rich nodded.

Who's your best friend? I asked him.

Terry Swanson, he said.

Terry Swanson, I said. He's Bobby Swanson's boy, is that
right?

I don't know, Rich said.

Okay, I said. I got the telephone book out and looked up
Bobby Swanson's number. I dialed him and he answered. Hey
Bobby, I said, are ya'll busy tonight?

No sir, Bobby said. Think it's going to be a pretty lazy night
around here.

Good deal, I said. Listen, Judy and me were talking, and Rich
hasn't gone to a sleepover yet. We haven't had a night alone in I
don't know how long.

Ben, my wife said to me.

Yeah, Bobby said. I think we could swing that. I heard him
call into the other room and check with his wife. We can do that, he
said. Bring the little guy over after while.

After I hung up Judy was standing there with this dirty look.
Why would you do something like that? she said.

Because I said, he's seven years old. He's a boy. Seven-year-
old boys go to sleepovers.

She walked away in a huff. I got a drink out of the fridge and nodded at Rich to go with her. When he left I popped the top and took a long drag. I could hear Judy sobbing in the boy's room.

I finished the beer and went in there. She was sitting on Rich's bed and crying into her hands. Rich sat in the floor at her feet.

Richie boy, I said to him. Pack yourself a bag.

He lifted himself up and got his backpack and filled it with a shirt and a pair of socks.

Here, Judy said, stopping and giving me another look, let me help, honey.

An hour later we were all in the kitchen. Judy was kneeled down and buttoning Rich's coat. You know, she said to him, you don't have to go if you don't want to.

Rich turned and looked at me and then back to her. I'll go, he said.

All right, she said. You go, and if you need anything you just call, okay? You feel bad, you get scared, anything at all, you can call me.

Jesus, I said. It's a sleepover.

Lay off, she said, touching Rich's hair. He needs to know I'm here.

Believe me, I said, he knows you're here.

Rich and I went to the car then and we drove ten minutes across town to Bobby's house. It was a brick place with a big flag flying in the front yard. We were halfway up the drive when Bobby and his son Terry came out the door. Terry ran over to Rich and me and gave Rich a little punch on the arm.

You ready to spend the night? he said.

Sure, Rich said.

How's it going? Bobby said.

Good, I said. Thanks again, I said.

No problem, Bobby said. We were just saying the other day that we should have Rich over.

He's excited, I said. Aren't you, buddy?

Rich was too busy talking to Terry to hear.

I think he's excited, I said.

Bobby and me talked for a minute or two while the boys ran inside. Then I told Bobby thanks again and backed out of his driveway. I figured I'd let Judy calm down some before I went home, so I cruised over to my buddy Steve's place. Steve was a guy I worked with. A bachelor and a good guy. His was the place everyone went to hang out or get high and drunk. It's an open door policy, he said one time.

I walked in and found him sitting in his living room, messing around on his guitar and watching TV. We got us a seat in there, me and him, and he got me a beer and then we started passing around this number.

How's business? I said, taking that number from him.

Good, he said. Good as always. Not doing much of anything.

Sounds great. I inhaled a big puff and tried not to cough. That sounds like the best of all worlds, I said.

You got it, he said and grabbed his guitar. He strummed out a few notes. How's everything on your end?

Shit, I said. Just dropped Rich off at a friend of his' house. It's his first sleepover.

That's always a good time, Steve said. He leaned over and took the joint from me and examined it. Me and my buddies used to spend the night at each other's houses all the time.

Yeah, I said. Stay up watching movies and bullshitting.

That's right, Steve said. He puffed at the joint and then puffed again. Say, he said, speaking of movies, you want to see some fucked-up shit?

The smoke was rolling around in my head and it sounded like something I wanted to do. So Steve put down his guitar and passed the joint again and then went over to where his TV was. He pulled a movie out and loaded it into his player.

I'm telling you, he said, I saw this the other day and it liked to have fucked me up.

Steve pushed a few buttons on his remote and that movie came on. But it wasn't a movie really. It was more of a collection of messed up videos. Some of them were of people taking big falls. There were skateboarders and bike riders and daredevils taking these spills. They'd get hurt bad, so bad you see their arms hanging the wrong way or bones sticking out of their legs.

Here, Steve said as a new video started, watch this.

In the new video a window-washer was working on the side of a skyscraper. He was on a scaffold way up in the colorless sky. Whoever was holding the video camera zoomed in on him and you could see the scaffolding was falling apart.

Here it is, Steve said.

Just as he finished saying that, the scaffolding gave way and that window-washer went tumbling through the air. He was falling, swinging his arms like he was trying to fly. He was falling and then he wasn't. He hit the sidewalk below and that was that.

Can you believe it? Steve said to me.

Holy shit, I said. I couldn't believe it. That pot had me to a place where I couldn't believe it.

We watched some more of that movie until I looked up and realized I needed to get home. Judy's pissed as is, I said. Need to get heading.

Tell you what, Steve said. You want to borrow this thing?

He had it out and was holding it. It was right there. I said sure.

And you know what? Steve said, pulling an unsmoked joint from his pocket. Here, it's on the house. Have yourself a night.

I took that video and joint and hid them in the glovebox of the car. At that point I was stoned as could be, a little buzzed too, so I was careful the whole way home. Made sure I followed all the speed limits, stopped at all the red lights.

When I got home Judy was sitting there in the kitchen, the way she always did. I want you to know, she said, that that was an asshole thing to do.

Lay off, I said. The boy needs to live a little.

I just want you to know that that's what I think, she said. I think that's a real asshole thing to do. I think you're acting like a real fucking asshole.

All right, I said. That's your opinion.

Judy slapped her hands on the table. This is supposed to be a partnership, she said.

What's done is done. I got a beer out and opened it. We've got the night off. We should enjoy it.

She sat there and I thought, for a second, it was like a light had gone off. She realized I was right and smiled.

We can live it up, I said, pulling out the joint Steve had given me. Like the old days.

Is that a joint? Judy said.

Yes ma'am, I said, holding it like I was a spokesmodel on a game show.

Ben, she said, I don't know if I'm comfortable with that.

Why not? I said. It's not like you never smoked.

She laughed then, the kind of laugh she would have laughed before she had Rich.

I don't know what it was, but seeing her like that lit me up. I went over to where she was sitting at the table and put my arms around her. First I squeezed her and then I snaked my hand up and over her shoulder and down into the front of her shirt.

Benjamin, she said.

Judith, I said.

We went and got into bed. We were together, really together, for the first time in ages. It was just like the old days, the two of us paying attention to each other in ways I'd forgotten about, and when it was over we were both sweaty messes and panting.

That was good, she said to me.

Uh huh, I said back.

Then we were getting rinsed up in the shower. Back in the day we used to only shower together. If I tried to go in there by myself she'd sneak in and give me a look like I was trying to pull something over on her. We were in there, lathering up, and we got started again.

I don't know what's got into me, she said afterwards, toweling off.

I know what's got into you, I said, and she gave me a playful push.

In the kitchen again, we got out some frozen dinners and heated them all up. There was lasagna and Mexican food and pizzas and we made it all and spread it out on the table like it was some kind of low-rent Thanksgiving.

What're we going to do with all this food? she said.

We're going to eat it, I said, jabbing a fork into a mound of rice.

We took the food into the living room and camped out on the couch. I sparked that joint and we passed it back and forth a few times. Judy would take a puff and then hold it out, examine it, and then hit it again.

This is crazy, she said. Just madness.

I turned on the TV and flipped around. There wasn't anything on, so I said to her, Hey, listen, my buddy Steve was showing me this movie.

What kind of movie? she said.

I told her what kind. She seemed scared.

She said, You mean these are real videos?

The real deal.

Oh my god, she said. I can't believe that's something that exists.

It does, I said. Should we watch it?

Judy put down the plate of food she was eating and seemed to really consider it. I'm curious, she said. I'm really, really curious.

I couldn't believe it, I said. It was that crazy.

All right, she said. She was nodding hard. We should watch it. That's something we should watch.

I said okay and went to get the movie in the kitchen. When I got back she was puffing on that joint again.

I'm nervous, she said.

I put the video in and pressed play. Back on the couch, she got close, like we were about to watch a horror movie or something, and I put my hand back down the front of her shirt. You got me, I told her.

Judy smiled and nuzzled happily into my shoulder.

The video played the scenes I'd watched before. There were the falls, the injuries, and every time someone went down Judy would flinch. Then we got to the window washer.

What's going to happen to him? she asked.

Just watch, I said.

Is he going to fall? she said. Holy shit, he's going to fall.

Calm down, I said. Just watch. Let it happen.

The scaffolding fell apart then and the window washer went tumbling through the sky. His arms flailed like I'd seen before. He hit the ground and the camera focused on the spot where he'd hit.

Oh fuck, Judy said, jumping off the couch, her hands on her face. Was that real?

Hundred percent real, I said, reaching to hit the joint again.

That's crazy, she said. That can't be real. Oh my god. Oh my god. That can't be real.

I think it's real, I said. The movie had moved onto a car accident. A little hatchback and a truck had hit head on and the drivers were both dead. There was glass and blood everywhere, police standing off the side. Hey, I said to Judy, still standing there in disbelief. Let's watch, I said.

Oh god, she said. She was pacing back and forth across the floor. Ben, she said to me, tell me that's not real.

I hit the pause button on the remote. What? I said.

Ben, she said, tell me this is a fake movie. Please.

What're you going on about? I said.

Oh god, she said again. Ben, I've got to make a phone call.

She disappeared into the kitchen and I heard her fumbling through the drawers. Then I heard what could only be the phone book slapping against the counter. What's that guy's name? Judy said to me.

Who? I said.

The kid Rich's staying with, she said. She was back in the living room now, looking heated. What's his name, you sonuvabitch?

Whoa, I said, hold on here.

Goddamn it, she said, what in the hell is the name of the kid Rich is staying with right now? What's his name? Where the hell is my boy?

I got off the couch and went into where the phone book was in the kitchen. In her panic she'd ripped a few pages out and they lay in scraps on the floor. Here, I said, pointing to Bobby Swanson's number. But I don't know what the big deal is...

Get the fuck out of the way, Judy said, grabbing the phone and dialing the number. She waited while it rang and looked at me like I'd killed somebody. Why would you upset me like that? she said. Then, into the phone, Hello, she said, hi, this is Rich's mother Judy. Hi, okay, listen, she said. Is Rich all right?

Judy, I said.

Put him on the phone please, she said and then put her hand over the receiver. Fuck you, she said to me. Fuck you, you awful sonuvabitch.

Hey, I said. What?

Hi honey, she said into the phone. How are you? You okay, honey? Okay. Okay. Listen, she said, I'm going to come pick you up, okay? All right? Pack up your bag, honey. I'll be there soon. Okay. I love you. I love you. Bye.

She hung up the phone and tore out the page with Bobby Swanson's number and address. She crumpled it in her fist and shoved me with it.

You listen here, she said to me. What the hell is wrong with you?

What the hell is wrong with you? I said. What's this all about?

I want you gone when we get home, she said. Gone and out of sight.

With that, she grabbed the keys to the car and took off. I didn't know what to do, so I sat on the couch and hit the play button again. The joint was only half-smoked, so I took a pull and a drink of my drink. The movie was to a new scene with a group of hunters. One had mistaken another for a deer and shot him in the chest. He was lying on the ground, his blood seeping into the dirt.

I'm sorry buddy, one of his friend's was saying. He still held the gun in his hands. Buddy, he said, I'm so sorry.

Judy came home with Rich a little while later. It was twelve-sixteen. I'll always remember that. Rich looked like he'd been woken up. There were lines on his face from a pillow. Judy marched him straight to bed and closed the door behind them. Two hours later, the joint gone, all the beer gone, the movie over, I went to see what was what. I opened the door. The light was still on. They were both on his bed, Judy wrapped around him, her arms keeping him close. I said Judy, but if she heard me she didn't let on.

I did the only thing I could do. I went and sat back down. I started that movie over. There were all those folks hurting themselves, but I fast-forwarded. That's not what I was looking for. That's not what I wanted to see. I got back to that part with the window washer. I watched the camera close in on him as he ran that squeegee across the glass. He was so far up that his face was a blur. I watched him in those seconds before, how he was just doing his job, just carrying on like normal, and I thought of how calm and clear it must've been up there. Then I looked down at his feet. Down at the scaffolding. I watched them bow and shift and I watched them come apart.

LOVELY LAND

By god, he yelled, the way you love I'd be better off in the wilderness.

It was a proclamation he offered often and his lover Sweet Pea had no understanding. He'd lectured to her on the inherent privilege of the male sex, the unbalanced transaction of love – the female a bearer of beautiful antiquities and the male a basket of half-rotted fruit – but no matter how he explained it, how loud he grew in tone, she would shake her head and assure him the matter was square.

I'm afraid you don't listen, he told her in the parking lot of the Piggly Wiggly. The shape and heft of your love is crushing me, consuming me, threatening to swallow me whole. He was pulling at the thighs of his denim. If I don't leave town, he said, leave this bed of lust and seek penance, I'm as good as dead.

Having recently moved her every possession into Tupelo's apartment by the park, Sweet Pea was reasonably distressed. In the throes of their passion he had regularly promised her forever, even an existence beyond forever he had taken to calling Lovely Land, until recently when the intensity had seemingly grown too free and too wild and their coupling was to be followed by violent ruminations on Tupelo's part. After they had come undone he walked the four rooms of his apartment, banging his fists and still-hard member against the walls, his cries that of a guilt-soaked beast.

Why? she asked as she tried to soothe him and stroked his sweat-silked hair. She existed to live and to help Tupelo live, the kind of partnership she had dreamed of, the kind that she had been told was only a myth or artifact of folklore. When he shivered and gnashed his teeth, so hard at times that bits of them broke off like gravel, she responded by squeezing him harder to her breasts and sweetening her voice to new and unheard of levels.

Because, he said to her in those moments, because.

His mantra, his enchantment, he said it again in the packed lot of the Piggly Wiggly, a rucksack waiting on the hood of his car. Because, because, because. He looked out across the highway and then pointed at a clove of trees. The Bulloch County State Forest. Forty square miles of every manner of southern tree and southern beast. That, he said to her, is where I belong. With my brethren of dirt.

Sweet Pea was about to beg him one last time, to bare her heart and remind him of the love she carried like so much weight, but he was hustling toward the trees, toward the waiting lap of steaming nature. He crossed the highway, a stream of hustling cars separating him and Sweet Pea, so much that when he looked back, a lusting wife of Lot, he saw only the marquee of the grocery store, the towers in the distance, the life he'd left behind.

The first night he camped two miles in and prepared a meal of beans and half a loaf of bread. While the beans finished on the fire he laid out the last vestiges of his former existence. He had brought along, for good measure, the Semi-State patch he'd earned as a lineman for the Bulldogs his junior year of high school, a single thread from a quilt his dearest grandmother had made him, and four photos of Sweet Pea, their surfaces already teeming with cracks and wrinkles.

Oh, he said to those pictures, the group of them spread about the fallen log he'd taken to using as his coffee table, Sweet Pea, if only you knew you were the sweetest succubus of them all.

It was a paranoid delusion he was having difficulty unknotting from reality. One night, after a marathon session, he'd lay awake in his bed next to a snoring Sweet Pea and stared at the ceiling until he'd been privy to a vision. He remembered lying there and thinking, If I stare long enough, if I think hard enough, then surely the Eye of Existence will open to me.

And sure enough it had. Amid a whirling, glowing stew of lights the Eye had opened and Tupelo's every paranoia had been confirmed. He saw amid the vision the very god and savior of Flesh, a pink and glistening idol that groaned and screamed in agonistic ecstasy with its every movement. Behind him, ready to be unleashed, an army of trained succubae and steely-eyed assassins of sex. Among them, highly decorated and in a position of leadership, his one and only Sweet Pea.

Sleep eluded Tupelo that night as the raw power of his hallucination overloaded his circuits and left him in a wordless stupor. Even when Sweet Pea rose up from the bed, stretching and straightening her dangerously perfect body in the sunlight, he was left without so much as a good morning. She walked into the bathroom and, within his full view, teasingly prepared for her day.

In the midst of the display Tupelo knew what he had to do. He had to leave. He had to run into the great yonder and fast the way a holy man would. He had to find a place devoid of stimulation or temptation and purify himself of the delicious toxins she'd loosed into his bloodstream.

He slammed his fist into one of the pictures – a snapshot of him and Sweet Pea lounging on the beach, the two of them holding cold longnecks and smiling, Tupelo remembering the sweet session they'd shared that very morning as a neighbor clicked the camera. Then he battered it again for good measure. A knot in the log under it bruised his hand and when he raised it up for inspection he could see that he'd also ripped the skin and left a small riverbed of blood. He pressed it to his mouth and sucked until it offered no more.

My blood, he thought, spitting it on the ground. A sacrifice to the wild.

As he did he felt a pinch somewhere above his ankle. Then another. A few pinches began on his other calf. He stood up, alert, already feeling the power of nature and the certainty of his plan. To witness it further he pulled up the legs of his jeans and saw dozens of tiny red dots roaming up and over his skin, through the curls of his dark hair, an army of fire ants feasting on him.

Tupelo raised his arms and bellowed, Savior of Flesh, your message is received.

He let the fire ants get their fill until the itching grew so terrible that he had to reach down and swat them away. His legs were covered in tiny welts and the itch was so overwhelming he sat down on the log and got to work scratching, his fingernails digging deep, deep into his skin and burrowing until the itch, if only temporarily, was satisfied.

That night he slept in fits, a consistent dream haunting him. In it, Sweet Pea and her battalion of temptresses laid Tupelo upon a bed of fine linens and stroked fistfuls of spices into his skin. Sweet

Pea, directing them, pointed out every inch bare of attention and then brought her mouth into full view for Tupelo and told him it was time. With a great grunt Sweet Pea and company lifted Tupelo into the air and carried him through a jungle of wet palms and over a raging mad sea. Tupelo tried to break free but found himself a powerless victim to their whims. The procession entered into another wild patch and then a clearing where more women, each more beautiful than the last, beat on drums and played handmade flutes and whistles, their song building until Tupelo was forced to hold his ears to keep them from bursting. In his delirium he nearly missed the temple ahead, the stones stacked on top of one another into a perfect, leveled pyramid. Up the steps Tupelo was carried until they reached a platform that stood high above the clouds. He was laid out, stretched and bound, Sweet Pea hovering above him with a sharpened glint of onyx, seemingly waiting for someone, or something, to join them.

Tupelo woke from the terror. He was still in the forest, still lying on a bed of pine needles. His body was wracked in pain, sore, the bites crying and screaming out in agony. He grabbed the nearest rock and pressed it into the bites until they opened and bled. His mouth was full of his tongue, swollen so large he could barely work up spit or swallow, and when he reached in to feel it was like an organ he didn't recognize.

My god, he yelled out into the night, the words muffled by his engorged tongue. Bring me another vision.

Shortly after he passed out and was woken only by the morning sun breaking through a thin layer of clouds. When he opened his eyes he was aware of a whole other level of suffering. Over the course of the night his joints had locked into place and his tongue had continued to grow until it was so large and bloated it hung out over his lips. He touched the end of it and found it dry, nearly solid. Even worse, the air around his eyes glowed with the same lights that had illuminated his vision earlier. They were crowding in from the corners and threatening to consume everything.

The realization came upon Tupelo in short order that he was dying.

Wasting away in the uncaring womb of the world.

He extended a shaking hand and clawed with all of his strength into the dirt. He pulled himself forward. His other hand. Another few inches. He was crawling away, leaving his rucksack, his provisions, his spent can of beans and half-empty sack of bread. Food, he knew, was of no use to him now.

In his head he did the calculations. Two miles. Just far enough that he would die before he saw any glimpse of civilization. He made it forty feet and rested. The scab that his body had become whistled in pain. He rested his face in the dirt and then remembered the pictures he'd left behind. Death was a certainty now, a foregone conclusion, and in his moment of perfect agony he knew if he perished he wanted to perish while gazing on Sweet Pea's visage.

Three hours passed. He crawled the forty feet back and lifted his body up and onto the log. It was swaying with the wind, an instrument he no longer controlled. The pictures were spread out over the pine needles, where he'd thrown them in a delusional fit the night before. The closest was the one of them on the beach. He, hoisting his beer into the air, the sun glinting off the metal, Sweet Pea lying back, ever the calmer of the two, her bountiful harvest glistening in its own right. He looked at the picture as the lights began to swarm closer to one another. He squinted and remembered the smell of her sweat that day as she cooked in the sun.

There was a noise somewhere in the woods. Tupelo heard it but was unable to look. He'd lost nearly all motor function and had been reduced to a decoration on the forest floor. Instead, he stared at the picture and remembered how they'd talked about Lovely Land that day. Lovely Land, he'd said as the waves roiled into their feet and then retreated.

The noise approached Tupelo. It was only eight feet away, nine at the most. He forced his neck to strain and lift his insubordinate head to gaze in its direction. He saw a figure through the fog of lights, a figure on two legs with a pair of outstretched arms. He saw Sweet Pea, coming for him, beckoning him, calling him home.

With every bit of remaining energy, Tupelo raised shakily off of the log. At last he would go to her. He would conquer the fear, damn the visions, and lie within her sweet embrace once and for all. If love, he thought, was a pyramid in the clouds, a razor-sharp stone to the gut, then love it was. Let love in, he thought. Love. Love. Love.

Struggling against himself, he leapt into the waiting arms. He tossed his body, devoid of any and all worry or fear and his body, weak and loose like a doll's, hurdled through the fresh air, his flesh suddenly alive, his member, bespeckled in pulsing bites, rallying one last call to action. He joined her, that growling, drooling monster of a brown bear, his loins pulsing and grinding, if only out of instinct alone.

STARE AT THE SUN

Rob and Linda had hit a lull. The love they had shared for over ten years was waning and the future looked bleak. There were conversations that lasted well into the night, bouts of begging and pleading and crying that left them hopeless and tired. Couples therapy sessions degenerated into desperate shouting matches and bruised feelings. It seemed as if it was about time to call it quits, to face the ugly truth and say goodbye.

The genesis of this crisis was a party the two had attended the winter before. An artist friend had hosted an ironic Anti-Christmas party in the ironic cottage home he shared with his ironic wife Maybel. The house, a cozy brick hamlet, was decorated in all of the normal trimmings: tinsel, bows, trees with dazzling star-toppers. Smiling cutout Santa Clauses taped to every door below dangling clusters of mistletoe. There were bowls of punch and egg-nog over which Rob and Linda and their intellectual friends hovered and shared knowing winks and amused glances.

Merry Christmas, the artist said, wrapping his arm around his ironic wife Maybel's waist, drawing her in for an ironic kiss. Good fortune and good cheer, he said, pausing for laughter and sarcastic applause.

It was the type of party Rob and Linda loved. They glided through the room, hand in hand, making small talk with the professors and performance artists they had met at previous ironic holiday parties. They discussed the death of art and public school funding and The Right's attack on reproductive care.

If they had their way, Rob said to no one in particular, we'd all be voting for Goldwater and chugging downtown in our Model-T's.

And watching Joan Cleaver after supper, Linda added.

The artist and his ironic wife Maybel and all their intellectual friends liked Rob and Linda a good deal. They were funny, smart, and the permanence of their love and monogamy made them feel better about their difficulties in that particular discipline. It seemed there was nothing in the dark and uncaring world, no pessimistic force, that could wedge between the pair and suffer their bond.

That was before Brewster Hogan though.

Brewster was a lecturer at the nearby private college and considered a rising star among the company of friends Rob and Linda kept. He arrived to the artist's parties later than everyone and left after only a few minutes. He wore hound's-tooth, head to toe, and he made a production of cutting down the artist and his ironic wife Maybel and all their friends. He smoked cheap cigarettes and ruined whatever good cheer there was by raising intolerably depressing ideas that were both soul-crushing and undeniable in their truth.

I teach my students the relationship between Christ and Santa Claus, he began that night. It was three hours into the party and he was standing, smoking and spilling tobacco on the floor under one of the ironic Santa Claus cutouts. I tell them that Christ is like the single-mother. Selfless, martyring, bleeding on a cross and offering intangible things like hope, forgiveness, unconditional love.

I hate him, Rob whispered to Linda by the ironic punch bowl.

Not now, Linda said. I want to hear this.

And I tell them, Brewster continued, that St. Nick appears once a year like a forgetful, rejuvenated, mid-life-crisis-yoked father, bearing gifts and tooth-rotting candy. A spoiling parent unable and completely unwilling to deal with consequences or intangible things. He is the reality we have chosen and he is who we ultimately love because we are, ourselves, incapable of fathoming a future, dealing with consequences, or of loving anyone or anything other than ourselves.

The monologue drew a smattering of nods from the more nihilistic guests and the rest gathered in clusters to simultaneously damn and admire Brewster. Rob refused to give the spewings any credence. Dime-store philosophy, he said to a nearby Linguistics Chair. A tried and true rant against commercialism that any freshman worth his salt could compose.

He turned to Linda for support, but she wasn't there. What he found was a PhD candidate with a handful of sweaty dissertation pages. I've been saying this for years, he cried, hair standing on end. Geraldo Rivera is John the Revelator, he said. Diane Sawyer the Whore of Babylon.

Rob excused himself hurriedly and searched the party for Linda. Aside from their respective employment and time spent reading journals and letters in their studies, they were never more than a few inches apart. This separation felt wrong and dangerous.

The partygoers were coalescing then, breaking down from their small groups and cliques, the Marxists and Deconstructionists and Feminists clotting into a wild, frenzied pack in the artist's living room. Theory shot through the air and collected like invisible strands and gained heft and weight and then disappeared just as quickly. Everyone clamored for Rob and Linda to refute Brewster's claim, to take his black hole and reverse its polarity.

Give us light, they seemed to say.

Here's what I know, Rob said, swimming through in search of Linda.

The crowd hushed. They waited.

Rob opened his mouth.

He could not answer.

Sick in his gut, Rob left the crowd in confusion and fought his way into the kitchen. The walls were painted an ironic sea-foam green and decorated with typical, ironic, Midwestern-kitchen pictures of fruits and vegetables. Above the sink a plaque that read HOPE, FAITH, FAMILY, LOVE. The artist and his ironic wife Maybel stood under it, the both of them looking shocked. A few other guests joined them. Over by the microwave, an ugly model from the Seventies bought on clearance at a pawnshop, was Linda. There, his hand holding loosely his ill-rolled cigarette, by her side, was Brewster Hogan. He was leaned over, his snake of a tongue darting in and out of Linda's ear, like a cat probing the bottom of an ice cream bowl.

The ride home was tense for Rob and Linda. Rob seethed in his anger as tears of wrath dripped down his face. Linda was busy with her own resentment. Rob had interrupted what had been, for her, a revelatory moment. Brewster's advances had felt like a loosening of chains she hadn't even known she'd struggled with. His wet tongue like the whisper of some all-powerful being.

I found myself, she said to Rob in the car. You may hate it, but the second I felt the spit and warmth I knew I'd been living a lie.

A lie? Rob said.

A lie, Linda said. Humans are complex animals capable of so many physical and emotional sensations. Monogamy and isolated-love are illusions. Punishments dreamed up by the Puritans and the Disney Corporation.

For days they fought over the ramifications of such a change. Linda spent her afternoons lounging in the backyard, naked, tanning her body in the sun and reading of surgical mishaps. Rob carried loads of pictures out to her in hopes it might help to ease the tide. They were snapshots of the two of them, candid moments of love and appreciation.

I look so young, Linda said, turning over so that her rump and back might catch some color. So naïve. So hopeful.

In a week's time a card arrived in the mail addressed to Linda. Brewster Hogan had sent it, a store-bought note meant for someone bereaved at the passing of a mother. On the front a picture of a vase full of lilies, the words I'm So Sorry For Your Loss. In it he had written, in barely legible writing, *I do not now, nor will I ever, love you as a person or a construct. Thank you, however, for lending me your delicious canal.*

Rob flew into a rage. From the built-in shelves of the living room he ripped their books into the floor and tore a good deal of pages. He grabbed their specially ordered wine glasses from the cabinets in the kitchen and smashed them against the wall. Linda rolled outside in the grass like a dog, the card either grasped in her hands or placed carefully in the dirt by her face. Each explosion of anger or despair from the house seemed to further her ecstasy.

She slept with the card under her pillow. She read it aloud all hours of the night. When Rob asked her to stop, or why should wouldn't move out, she told him that the rot of their love was beautiful, as beautiful as a carcass on the side of a road.

I can't do this, Rob said. I'm losing my mind.

Yes, Linda said, pulling her shirt up and touching her own skin. More, she said.

I'm hollowed out, Rob said. No good for anything.

Yes, Linda said, working the button on her jeans. Don't stop.

He begged her all day and night. Love me or leave, he said. He drug her to counseling and the doctors and therapists listened and wept.

My entire practice, one said, a complete lie. I am a charlatan, an impotent physician.

Please, Rob said again. Love me or leave.

Months passed. Linda did not leave. She quit her employment and drank hard liquor and rolled naked in the grass. She took lovers and made them recite the card during their lovemaking. I do not now, nor will I ever, love you as a person or a construct, they said. She begged Rob to make love to her and recite the card. Sometimes, in moments of weakness and desperation, he did.

I do not now, nor will I ever, he said, love you as a person or a construct.

No, Linda said. But you do. You do.

I do, he confessed.

Rob fell into a stupor. Each day seemed more unfair and brutal than the last. Sometimes Linda left long screeds posted to the bathroom mirror. In them she coldly and intellectually broke down those things she had believed to love about Rob and dissected how societal influences and learned norms had caused those delusions. Several were published in notable journals and reviews and Linda read from them at universities. Rob sat there, in the front row, trying to manage a smile while holding a cup of water and pretending as if his world wasn't collapsing.

The artist threw more parties. He and his ironic wife Maybel and their intellectual friends urged Linda and Brewster Hogan to lecture.

Valentine's Day, Linda would say, is akin to a slaughter. The cattle fatted on lies and prepackaged affection. Their hooves fitted with rings-turned-sickles and the jugulars tied with lacy bows.

The hearts are telling, Brewster returned. We are invited to feast on our partner's organs and find ourselves caked in their blood and sated.

Rob did his best to listen, but when talk turned to rotted genitals and the false hope of antibiotics he hurried to the bathroom and relieved himself of all the ironic-punch and ironic-candies he'd gorged on earlier in the night. He stayed there on the tile floor, admiring the ironic-rug that sat there and read HOME SWEET BOWL. From the other room came a quick applause and the buzz of discourse. He knew Linda and Brewster had concluded and threw up again.

As he rose from the floor, he saw a peculiar book on the back of the toilet. It was called *Stare At The Sun* and had a picture on the cover of a bone broken in half. A Dr. Harvard Rocket had written it, and on the back was his picture. His eyes were blackened and his hand outstretched. In his palm a pile of bloody teeth.

Rob flipped through the pages and saw it was a self-help volume, the kind that lined the shelves at the local big-box bookstore he regularly avoided. The chapters had titles like Admire Your Bruise and A Story About Pestilence. For no reason at all, Rob slipped the book under his shirt and tucked it into the waist of his pants.

From there he returned to the party and stood silently while a physicist educated at MIT tried to take Linda's rant about syphilis and tie it to his rejection of Newton's Laws and, eventually, Newton's very existence.

Later, in bed, while Linda rubbed Brewster's card over her body and moaned like a whale, Rob read through Dr. Rocket's book. He studied it word for word, page for page, and considered his options. He could escape into the night and run as far away from Linda and all their intellectual friends as he could and never look back. He could start a new life and try, for the rest of his days, to forget he'd ever loved Linda in the first place. Or, he could call the number listed in the notes of the book and make an appointment to see Dr. Rocket.

In the morning Rob woke at eight and made breakfast. He fried some fake-bacon and mixed it with some fake-eggs from the neighborhood co-op. With a glass of almond milk he washed it down. He offered Linda some, but she refused. She was heading to the backyard with her blanket and tanning oils. Her bikini was already untied and falling off. She had a book of architectural disasters in tow. Rob watched her lie down on the blanket and watched her remove Brewster's card from the book. Rob watched until he couldn't, and picked up the telephone.

Dr. Rocket's office, a woman answered. Are you having an existential crisis?

Yes, Rob said. The woman I love is possessed of love of death and celebration of destruction.

This happens all the time, the woman answered. Let's you get in to see Dr. Rocket. Okay?

Okay, Rob said and felt better than he had in months.

In a week he and Linda flew to the city to see Dr. Rocket. Linda had read *Stare At The Sun* and seemed to like it more than Rob had expected.

His story about his son, she said to him on the plane, is a thing of beauty.

It was awful, Rob said. The poor boy stood in a field and burned his eyes out. He looked at the sun until he was blinded.

Exactly, Linda said. I think it's wonderful.

There was a car waiting for them at the airport, a stretch limo with a spacious backseat and TVs lining the ceilings and walls. Each tuned to video of war and conflict. Buildings collapsed around Rob and Linda. Mortars fired and troops gathered their dead.

I feel sick, Rob said.

Don't turn away, Linda said, pointing to a close-up of rubble. It's part of the treatment.

Dr. Rocket's office was in the city's industrial section, where the buildings were dilapidated and tagged with graffiti. Hopeless people wandered the streets and looked wild. One man, homeless from all appearances, lay bleeding at the feet of a man wearing an expensive suit and carrying a club. The building the car pulled in front of had rusting doors and a sign that revealed it to be an abandoned meatpacking plant.

The inside smelled of frost and sweat. A woman in a smart business outfit greeted them. Rob recognized her voice from the phone call.

You must be Rob and Linda, the woman said. Dr. Rocket is so excited to see you.

She led them across the main floor and past out-of-use conveyor belts and dangling hooks. Rob, a long-practicing vegetarian, could picture large slabs of dripping meat hanging from the ceiling. The thought, mixed with his already-tired nerves, cramped his stomach and slowed his pace.

At the end of the floor was a door that led into a hallway. The walls covered in pictures and diplomas. Rob recognized the man in the pictures as Dr. Rocket. In them he was doing ordinary, everyday things: drinking coffee, eating a plate of spaghetti, playing catch with a beautiful child who looked like he belonged in catalogue pictures. The diplomas numerous and framed extravagantly, though Rob couldn't place any of the universities.

He's certainly qualified, Linda said.

Dr. Harvard Rocket is very well respected, the woman said, opening a door at the end of the hall. He has published impressively and has treated many famous clients.

The next room was a more traditional office. There were wooden bookcases and handsome volumes of books and journals. A grandfather clock stood in the corner behind an imposing, custom-made desk.

He'll be in to see you, the woman said, leaving Rob and Linda alone in the office.

They took the seats in front of the desk and tried to make themselves comfortable. Rob bit his fingernails and fidgeted while

Linda studied Dr. Rocket's desk and the pictures he kept there. They were the exact pictures that were hung in the hallway, with the exception of one: a portrait of a chubby-faced child wearing glasses, both the lenses blacked-out.

That's his boy, Linda said to Rob. The boy who stared at the sun.

Put it down, Rob said. I'm starting to think this is a bad idea.

Nonsense, came a voice that seemed to originate from inside one of the back walls. There was a whirring, like from a rusted motor, and a bookcase slid over to reveal a secret room. Come inside, the voice said. Rob and Linda obeyed and walked through the secret door, finding an office identical to the one they'd just been sitting in.

Behind the desk in that room was Dr. Rocket. He was seated in a wheelchair and most of his body encompassed in a cast. Spots of blood seeped through his bandages and when he talked they saw he was missing his front teeth.

Welcome Rob and Linda, he said. I can't tell you how much I've been waiting for today.

Me either, Linda said from the edge of her seat. I loved your book.

Yes, Dr. Rocket said. I read the introductory essay I assigned you. It seems you appreciated my anecdote about my overzealous son.

I did, Linda said.

Good, Dr. Rocket said. When my son came to me, sightless, I despaired. I said to my wife, the world is cruel to the blind. We wept. We prayed in our weakest moment. But, he said, I'll tell you something if you want.

Please do, Linda said.

Well, Dr. Rocket said, to hear my son's account of that day is to hear the real, honest truth. He said, Father, I stared at the sun because it was there. I'd seen it so many days from the corner of my eye that I couldn't look away any longer.

Poetry, Linda said.

About our appointment, Rob said.

The appointment, Dr. Rocket said. You paid in advance so I've given this a lot of thought, Robert. I've given the whole situation a lot of hard, hard thought.

What's your diagnosis? Linda said excitedly.

My diagnosis is that you are human, Dr. Rocket said. My diagnosis is that we humans try too hard not to notice strife and decay.

This isn't therapy, Rob said.

But it is, Linda said.

What you have to understand, Dr. Rocket explained, is that there are only two truths, Robert. We are born and we will die. Family and love and beliefs are inconsequential and merely by-products of suffering. The only recourse is violence.

More, Linda said, reaching over to make sure Rob couldn't leave.

Before you, Dr. Rocket said, apes and humans were hunted like gazelles, torn down midstride by predators and devoured raw and still breathing. Love meant large groups. Monogamy meant better odds of escape once the killers descended.

Rob sat in dumfounded shock and watched as Dr. Rocket pressed the control on his wheelchair and rolled over to Linda's side. Linda was wild at that point, her blouse hiked up and her slacks undone. Dr. Rocket carefully leaned toward her. She leaned closer and met him. His tongue came from behind his lips.

There is no morality, he said. No reason why I shouldn't insert my greedy tongue into Linda's ear.

None, Linda said.

Rob leapt from his chair as Dr. Rocket's tongue wiggled in. He gripped his fist and struck him hard on the cheek. Linda screamed and Dr. Rocket spit blood onto his cast.

Good, he said to Rob. You're learning to accept the limitations. The truth. You need to realize your beliefs are created and cannot keep you safe from death.

Accept it, a swooning Linda whispered.

Just as Linda here, Dr. Rocket said, moving in, must accept that her nihilism, her infatuation with suffering, is only another form of denial.

What? she said.

Dr. Rocket said, You and your sad-sack philosophy are as traditional and expected as songs about marriage and poetry. As normal as picking apples from an orchard.

Linda pounced on him then, slapping his face and wrenching his broken arms. The bones creaked and splintered, but Dr. Rocket continued. Seeking safety in a pack, he sang joyfully, is still seeking safety in a pack.

Rob joined her in tearing at Dr. Rocket's skin as he fell out of his chair and into the floor. He chanted, Stare at the sun, stare at the sun, stare at the sun, as Rob and Linda attacked him. Then he was coming apart, Dr. Rocket was, his body a husk that pried off easily in their hands, the two of them, Rob and Linda, together, wrestling from him his limbs and finally, finally, his pink worm of a tongue.

THE DEATH OF SECOND PERSON

You are you.

There is no one like you as you are composed of a lifetime of unique events that have shaped you.

After a fitful night of sleep, you slink into the bathroom and, for some reason, remember a class you took your sophomore year at Tennessee. The professor a stodgy old woman with scars on her face from where her horde of cats had attacked her over the years. You earned a C because you were too focused on sneaking into Rooster's every night and trying to master the fine art of underage drinking. It's one of the few black marks on your transcripts.

In social circles you explain it away, saying it was because you could never get behind dead forms of thought.

You are clever when you need to be.

When you walk by the mirror you think of the course and are reminded of the story of the young hunter who fell in love with his reflection. Narcissus. Or, as the scratch-laden professor insisted on calling him – Narkissos.

But as you scramble to remember tidbits of that failed education, the debris of it scattered across the dark ocean floor of your subconscious, you think of home. Of Huntsville, Alabama. Of the air drifting off The Gulf and your mother setting out pie tins full of cheap beer every night after supper.

In the morning you found them filthy with dead slugs. They drank so much they drowned. Kept drinking and drinking and drinking until they were nothing but bloated, crooked lines. Heads wrenching back to consume tails.

You don't fight it.

You look into the mirror.

You look into the mirror.

You.

Look into the mirror.

ALL THAT BREATHES AND CRAWLS

We rolled into Bloomfield on a Wednesday and parked next to the courthouse. We'd been driving pretty steady for days and needed some sleep. Rusty put on the radio and I asked him to look for some old country, some music about losing your love and wanting to go back home. He found a good one and we leaned our seats back and pulled our hats down to keep the sun out. It was wintertime and the world was mean.

After a couple hours we got out and had a stretch. We were on our sixth day and heading to Kansas City for Rusty's brother's wedding. The trip was supposed to take a day or two, but we got hung up in Dayton for three and the stops kept coming. Between the both of us we had ten or so bucks, just enough for a drop of gas or some pitchers of beer.

From the back of the car we got a couple of beers and poured them into some leftover coffee cups. We had a seat on a bench outside the courthouse and watched the good people come to pay their utilities and property taxes.

Sonuvabitch, Rusty said, and spit on the ground. Reckon we missed the ceremony.

A car pulled up and out stepped this old couple in matching sweaters and slacks. The wife had a neat little hat on with a ribbon on the side. She kept rifling through her purse and her husband wouldn't stop wiping his nose with a handkerchief.

I'm inclined to believe, Rusty said, that love is nothing but a disease.

I took a swig of my beer. It was warm. One could make a case, I said.

My wife says she loves me and curses my name in the same breath, Rusty said. She says I was put on this Earth to mystify and confound.

I get a letter from my boy every week, I said. And each is about how I am a curse he'll never escape. My shame is large and heavy.

We stuck around a bit and drank and watched the town move through its day. City trucks came by ever so often and salted the road. The sky got looking like snow too, what with the grey clouds and such.

I have one testicle, Rusty said. Was born with one and got only one to my name. It aches when weather's coming.

And now? I said.

Nearly crippling, he said.

We were fixing to leave when a police car parked in the spot next to ours. The officer opened his back door and pulled out a man in handcuffs. The officer led him down the sidewalk and right by us. I'd been there before, and lord knows I'll probably be there again, so I gave him a nod and wished him luck.

For lunch we found this little place across the street that sold breakfast all day. We both got some coffee and shared a stack of flapjacks. It was the most I'd eaten in weeks. I was so full I slumped down in the booth and let my belly hang out, all fat and satisfied.

Rusty felt pretty good too. He sat there across from me and picked his teeth awhile.

I got comfortable there, kicking my feet up and listening to forks scraping plates and spoons clinging against the sides of coffee cups. The waitress wasn't bad to look at either. Her name was Bernice and she smiled whenever Rusty or me said something smart.

That's the type of woman I could be happy with for the rest of my life, Rusty said after she'd refilled his cup. Something about the way she carries that pot tells me she's gentle. Patient and understanding.

He went on and on about how he was going to talk her into coming along to Missouri. How he'd have a pretty girl on his arm and show everyone what was what. But he didn't say anything to her besides thanks and thanks a lot. We cleaned up in the bathroom and went to get some more sleep in the car.

When we woke up snow and ice covered the windshield and the car was cold as hell. Night had set and the courthouse had concluded business. That town looked dead then except for a couple of restaurants and bars on the square. We chose the one with a neon sign in the shape of a guitar and went in to get warm.

Only people in the place was the bartender and a farmer in a mesh hat. He had a glass in front of him he kept staring at. For whatever reason he couldn't take his eyes off it.

Rusty got us a pitcher and I found a booth in the back where we wouldn't be bothered.

Bastard's half foam, Rusty said, pointing at the beer.

It's lukewarm, I said. Tastes like spit.

We drank and watched the snow come down. Some songs played on the jukebox, but the speakers didn't work right and the voices sounded fuzzy.

The rent is two weeks overdue, Rusty said. There's a stack of bills I haven't even looked at. I'm so deep I'll never get out.

I said, Every Sunday my mother calls and tells me how the cancer is eating her. She coughs and cries and prays.

My wife is in love with her neighbor, Rusty said. She calls whenever he trims his bushes and tells me how the sweat glistens on his back. He is perfect and she believes he could be in love with her too.

We finished the pitcher off and spent our last cent on another. It tasted as bad as the first, but we worked on it just the same. Outside it was getting ugly. Cars sliding through stops and running up on the sidewalk. After the farmer left it was just us and the guy working the bar for an hour or so. Then the door swung open and in stepped this fella wearing a thick Carhartt. He had on these real fancy-looking grey boots with red tips. He was older and carried this big pot stove of a gut that hung over his jeans.

How ya doin'? he asked the bartender. He grabbed a stool and pointed to the TV in the corner. Care to put the game on? he said.

The bartender clicked on the TV and went through the channels. Finally he came to a basketball game. The screen was full of static but I could see Indiana was playing Wisconsin.

Big game tonight, the bartender said.

No doubt, the fella said. We could play if we got our heads out of our asses and took care of the ball.

I left Rusty to his bitching and went up to watch. Wisconsin was tough and played the way a team should. They rebounded and fought through screens. They kept their heads in crunch time and never despaired.

Gonna have your hands full with them Badgers, I said to the fella.

That a fact? he said.

Sure is, I said. Indiana can't handle their press and they don't have the shooters.

The fella said, Hmm. Don't know if no one's told you or not, but you can't talk shit about the Hoosiers like that. Not around here. The fella lit up a smoke and ran his finger around the rim of his glass of beer. Boys been shot for less.

That a fact? I said. Well, I'll have you know I come from the Great State of Massachusetts, birthplace of the game, and I don't have to take shit from nobody.

The fella chuckled and took a sip. Fair enough, he said. Care to put a little money on the line?

Fifty, I said, feeling around my empty pockets. Got faith in those 'Consin boys. They're built like tractors and got arms like concrete posts.

The fella and me sat there and watched as Wisconsin got off to an eight-two start before hitting a cold stretch. Before I knew it it was half and I wasn't feeling so hot.

Looking good, the fella said. Looking real good. Say, figure we oughta put our money on the bar. Get the ugly business out of the way.

I moved around on my stool a little and felt the place in my jeans where my money'd be if I had any. Not to fixing to lose, I said.

I hear you, the fella said and polished off a glass and ordered another. Just don't want to think you might squelch, he said. That's all.

Soon as he said it I looked behind the bar where all the bottles of booze were lined up. There was a sign with a woman in a bathing holding a bottle in her hand. Below the sign was a shotgun with a filed down barrel.

Would just hate to think that, the fella said.

Rusty passed out on the table in the booth. Our pitcher was knocked over and the beer was spilling onto the floor. I knew if I had to make a run for the door I was gonna have to leave him behind and that made my heart sick.

Looky there, the fella said.

Wisconsin's star forward was lying at half-court, holding his knee and weeping. The coach loosened his tie and unbuttoned the collar of his shirt. The fans behind the bench cried and dug their nails into each other's flesh. The Hoosier faithful swooned and cried out in joy and deliverance.

After they carried the boy off the half started and things got worse. The Badgers looked shaken and lost the ball every time down the floor. The fella next to me cheered and pounded the bar. He kicked his special grey boots against the rungs of his stool. I kept looking at that shotgun.

This is about to get ugly, the fella said. U-G-L-Y.

But it didn't. All of a sudden those boys started working it inside and taking those close shots. The ones that didn't go in they grabbed off the cup and put them back in. Pretty soon they had a little seven-point run, then ten and then twelve. They chipped away until the lead was down to two and there was just fifty seconds on the clock.

I'll be damned, the fella said.

He didn't pound the bar no more and he didn't kick those boots around either. I'll be goddamned, he said as the Badgers tied the game up and settled into their press.

Right then I wanted to be on that court, wanted to be right there on the wing, the hot lights shining down and the people screaming. I'd seen the Hoosiers run a play the whole game, the guard cutting across the paint and getting the ball. I knew it was coming, sure as shit, and I knew if I was in there, Badgers written cross my chest, I could just float over and get a hold of that pass. I knew it like I knew my own name.

And goddamn if it didn't happen just like that. That point guard made his move and called for the pass, but that Wisconsin forward and me were on the same page. He left his man and jetted into the lane. The pass came and he got a finger on it, just enough to send it bouncing to the other block, right to the waiting hands of his teammate. I jumped and hooted as they went down court and rattled one in.

The fella didn't waste any time slapping five bills on the bar and making for the door. I picked up the cash and stuffed it in my pocket. It was the most money I'd had in years, and right then I thought of all the things I could do with it. I could spring for enough fuel to make Kansas City and even send my poor mother a few bucks to help with the pain. I could buy some paper and write my boy a letter that'd clear up all the misunderstandings. It would take care of all the space between us and maybe his shame would start to heal.

It took some effort but I shook Rusty awake and we had a couple of drinks before we headed out. The night was cold and the wind and snow stung, but we had bellies full of booze and money for some gas. The road was clear and Missouri seemed close enough to touch. We had a day of easy drive to go. Maybe three or four if we had a drink along the way.

OUR MOTHER, THE STAR

The apocryphal tale, of course, is that my mother was discovered pushing her cart down the baking goods aisle at the Piggly Wiggly in search of a cake mix for my older brother's birthday. The truth, if there's anything left of it, is that she was actually perusing the shelves for cupcake mix – strawberry cupcake mix, if we're going to be accurate – to make for her son who had just had a terrible, no-good day at school. I know because I was sitting in that cart when it happened and because I was that son.

She was reaching for that box when a man in a suit sprinted down the aisle covered in sweat, his face as red as a suffocating child's. Ma'am, he said, aiming his camera at my mother, are you aware that you are the most beautiful and perfect mother in all of the world?

My mother clutched her breast. She was obviously caught off-guard. The commotion of the man in the suit accosting us had filled her with noticeable dread. I'm sorry, she said. What?

From where I was in the cart I watched the agent circle us and take more pictures. He occasionally reached a shaking hand toward her, his body language screaming that he had somehow come across a holy relic, his eyes mad with fire. I'm from Hollywood, he declared, his voice similarly quaking. You are what we have sought after for decades now. Come with me. Make your fortune. Make my fortune. Please, he screamed. I beg of you.

That night the family gathered around the supper table. My mother had made pork and green beans, a ceramic bowl filled with glowing yellow corn. There were my brother and I in our customary seats, our father at the head of the table. He was beaming, smiling so hard it looked to have hurt. You're going to be a star, he kept saying. The biggest star I ever saw.

Stop, Mother said, embarrassed by all the attention. I don't even know if I want to do it, Frank. A commercial? She had just set the pork on the table and was busy shaking her head as if the idea was nonsensical. That's not me, she protested. I just can't imagine it.

Then imagine it, Father said. You have to. Imagine the possibilities. Imagine your face up on the silver screen.

Mother got a good chuckle out of that, as did Father and my brother. I didn't find the idea so humorous. After all, I hadn't received my cupcakes. In all the fuss Mother had forgotten the very mix we'd gone into the Piggly Wiggly to purchase in the first place. When the man had finally walked away she simply picked me out of the cart and abandoned it there in the aisle as we made our escape. In her hand was his card, which she stared at the entire way out to the parking lot, so much so that a Prairie Farms dairy truck nearly flattened us outside the door.

Mother, I said as she and Father and my brother laughed, I don't have my cupcakes.

She looked around the room as if they would be stowed away in the hutch or the armoire. Oh dear, she said. In all the fuss I forgot.

The tears began then. Just hearing the words spoken out loud was enough to send me over the edge and into a fit. That day, that terrible, no-good day, had been too much. Early in the morning, just after our first math lesson, Willy Billy Rose had stolen every last pencil out of my desk and snapped them in one wrathful movement. Before our teacher Mrs. Blowings could turn around he'd dropped them on the floor, loud enough to disrupt the problem on the board – if I remember correctly it was four apples minus one apple – and loud enough to gain Mrs. Blowings' attention. When she turned she saw only me and a pile of pencil rubble at my feet.

No recess, she'd declared without hesitation. No recess for the rest of the week.

I'd tried to protest but there was no use. When the bell rang and all of my classmates, Willy Billy Rose included, sprinted outside and climbed the monkey bars and swung in the swings, I was left to clean up the mess.

I'm so sorry, my mother said, trying to console me. We have ice cream in the fridge. I could run down to the gas station for a candy bar?

I didn't want ice cream.

I didn't want a candy bar.

The next week my mother went to Hollywood to film her first commercial. My father walked around the house, constantly humming and whistling like the happiest fool in the world. He made frozen dinners that were both scalding hot and bone-chillingly cold. My brother and I's lunches packed with plastic bags of chip dust and half-hearted peanut butter sandwiches. Home grew to be a dirty and cluttered place.

It wasn't until the following Sunday that Mother threw open the door and her arms and called us. When we ran to her we squeezed her until her breath was nearly stolen. I missed you, she said, I missed you, I missed you.

Maybe I was the only one to notice but something had changed. At first I couldn't quite pinpoint what it was, but then I realized it all in a snap. Her hair, normally a helmet of dirty blonde, was curled, styled, colored. Where it had once been nondescript, just a wig of hair that barely moved and reflected no light at all, it was now an expertly crafted persona all of its own. The light from our kitchen's fluorescents seemed to dazzle off it, like spotlights on the world's largest diamond.

And her scent had changed. It was like alcohol now, with subtle hints of berry and leather.

What's that smell? I asked. That smell, I said, something's different.

Oh, she said, that? A perfume I picked up while out west. It's from Paris.

Ooh la la, my father said and again the three of them laughed like they were in on the biggest joke that'd ever been told.

How was Hollywood? my brother asked.

Tell us about it, Father said.

It's a different world, my mother said, pulling her bags over to the couch. She let go of them and sunk into the cushions. Everything moves so fast, she said with a sigh. You barely have a moment to breathe.

What about the commercial? my father asked.

Yeah, my brother echoed, what about the commercial?

Producing a tape from one of her bags, Mother handed it to my father to slide into the player under the TV. After a few button presses the screen was filled with my mother, my glowing and radiant mother, done up to look like a goddess, pushing a grocery cart through the aisle of some unnamed and generic grocery store. In the basket of the cart a little boy of my age wearing a red and blue striped sweater, his hair blonde and possessed of a designed cowlick that served to let us know that he was just the slightest bit mischievous.

Look at you, Father said, turning from the screen to my mother, delirious in love and lust. Just look at you.

Mother, Brother said, you look so pretty.

Thanks, Mother said, blushing.

Is that supposed to be me? I asked, pointing at the boy in the cart.

Shush, Father said.

C'mon, my brother said.

The little boy with the cowlick pouted. Mother, I had the worst day at school.

Oh no, my mother said in the commercial. Her bright smile turned on a dime and transformed into a concerned frown. What happened?

I don't know, the little boy with the cowlick said and pouted. Teacher was mean to me.

Well, my mother said, what can I do to make it better?

The little boy with the cowlick considered the question. He even put his tiny little fist against his tiny little chubby cheek as if he were deep in consternation. My brother and father both made aww sounds as he did.

I want cupcakes, the little boy with the cowlick said and nodded as if he'd finally decided.

All right then, my mother reassured the little boy. Then cupcakes it is.

I watched her on the TV reach for the box of cupcake mix, the same brand that she always used to make cupcakes for me whenever I was sad or disappointed. Her nails were perfectly painted and perfectly manicured, the light glowing on them perfectly.

Then cupcakes it is, she repeated and held the box next to her face and paused to smile, her teeth so brilliant they hurt my eyes.

The scene shifted to a kitchen that was like ours but more up to date, more clean, more ideal. The little boy with the cowlick sat at the table, unwrapping an immaculate cupcake. He peeled the wrapper off slowly and savored what was bound to be the best cupcake he would ever have.

All better? Mother asked him as she held the pan.

The little boy with the cowlick held up the cupcake and smiled into the camera. All better, he said before taking a healthy bite.

The commercial closed and my father and brother clapped until I thought they might never stop. My mother hid her face in her hands and then looked up and asked if she'd done okay.

Award-worthy, my father said.

The best I've ever seen, my brother said.

I have to ask, I said. Was that supposed to be me?

Though my question was never answered, I received a trio of looks in return that told me the inquiry wasn't welcome.

Needless to say, the commercial took off. Mother was too all-American for it not to. Pretty soon everyone everywhere was eating cupcakes and wherever you went the catchphrase All Better started popping up. Kids said it in the lunchroom. On the playground. Even Willy Billy Rose, his face and fingernails dirty, his grin yellow and jagged, couldn't escape its power.

All better? he asked after he'd pushed me down in the gravel and dirt next to the slide.

I'd gone to Mrs. Blowings but she'd simply dusted off the knees on my jeans and then asked, in the most belittling way, All better?

I would've complained to Mother but she was absent by then. There were sequels to film to the All Better Campaign. She and the little boy with the cowlick became a hot commodity. At any given time you would see upwards of four or five variations of the commercial on the TV. In some it was vanilla, in some chocolate, in some strawberry, in some the boy had gotten in trouble with teacher and in some he'd struck out to lose a baseball game in gym class.

Everywhere All Better. At all times All Better.

The frozen dinners kept coming. Soon though, Father wasn't as cheerful. His humming and whistling faded away. Some nights he'd forget our dinners altogether and sit on the couch and watch Mother on the TV. The commercial would come to the part where she asked the little boy with the cowlick, All better? and Father, dejected and tired, would whisper, No. Just no. And yet Mother and the little boy with the cowlick would smile and then disappear into the ether as if it were all better.

Mother came home maybe once a month as the machine that was the All Better Campaign continued to chug along. The last time, the time before she disappeared for nearly two years, she was miserable, moody, quick to scream. Brother tried to show her a picture he'd drawn of her holding the pan of cupcakes – he'd spent the better part of a week on it, trying desperately to recreate her magic hair and megawatt smile, going over the lines constantly with his brightest yellow crayon and investing his allowance in different shades of white just to try and get the tone perfect – and she'd taken it into her manicured hands and ripped it to shreds. Brother had sat there on the floor, his legs crossed, his chest heaving, in disbelief as Father lifted Mother off the couch and took her in the other room for a long and, I assume, complicated talk.

Then, she disappeared. We didn't hear from her for eighteen months. She called Father one evening after three in the morning and told him, he told us, that she'd been filming a movie in Barbados and was bone-tired.

As Brother and I huddled at his feet, he begged her to come home. Come home and let's forget all of this business, he said.

No, I imagined her saying. I can't ever come home. It's too late. We're too far past home.

The movie came out the next year. Called THE ADVENTURE OF A LIFETIME, Mother was the love interest of a devil-may-care outlaw who made a living stealing precious stones from museums around the world. Father took us to the Saturday matinee. He was disheveled, near the point of throwing in the towel in regards to life and hope and love. I remember he'd taken to wearing the same red and blue striped sweater – a variant, I realized later in therapy, of the same sweater the little boy with the cowlick wore in the original All Better Campaign – every day until it smelled of body odor and the liquor he'd taken to drinking. Brother and I sat in our seats and when Mother appeared onscreen, wearing a tank top and sporting ridiculously chiseled arms, we both erupted into spontaneous crying jags. Father, so far gone, merely pulled the neck of his blue and red striped sweater over his face and either hid or wept, I can't quite recall.

She was on all the evening celebrity shows.

She was on all the red-carpet coverages.

She was on the news, rumored to be in disastrous but fantastical relationships.

She was on the magazines at the checkouts in the stores, rumored to be rumored.

Father gave up. I guess Brother did too. They slunk into a depression that consisted of closed doors and abbreviated grunts. I watched still, devoured every mention of Mother I could find. I was a glutton. When THE ADVENTURE OF A LIFETIME came out on video I rented it and watched it, frame by frame, until I couldn't. I was watching the penultimate scene, where the devil-may-care outlaw was about to turn over a new leaf and overcome his fear of commitment and took Mother in his arms and brought her close to his face and said, Never leave me? and she said, Never, and then they kissed a long and dangerous kiss while the music swelled, when Father erupted out of his room, slamming the door against the wall so hard the plaster fell like dust, and wrestled the player from under the TV and kicked it until it disintegrated into sparking parts.

The next day a long and gleaming black limousine appeared in front of our house. A driver in a tuxedo emerged and opened the back door. Mother glided out dressed to the nines in a fur and a sparkling ball gown. She was on her way to a benefit, she said, and wanted to stop in long enough to say hello. Father couldn't find the strength to protest. There wasn't enough time anyway. She was in the house all the longer it took for her to gesture at the driver to hand out the autographed pictures of herself to Father and Brother and me. In it she was still the all-American mother, only she was bejeweled with diamonds and rubies and necklaces of untarnished gold. TO MY BIGGEST FANS, the autograph read. LOVE, MOTHER.

I tried to explain to my wife years later what it was like to receive those pictures. I tried to explain how hollow I felt, how betrayed, as Mother and her driver left and reentered the gleaming black limousine. In an effort to be intimate and trust again I tried to relay what it was like to watch it glide on out of the neighborhood and disappear forever. But it was impossible.

We were trying to be honest. I had changed my name at that point as Mother had ruined it forever. My father and brother kept theirs but, from all I could tell, it only brought them more pain and torture when the news crews camped out on their lawn and shoved their microphones and cameras in their faces.

How does it feel? they asked them. How does it feel to know the most famous woman in all the world?

I couldn't handle another second more.

I got the autographed picture out and handed it to my wife. She examined it from every conceivable angle.

She looks perfect, she said without taking her eyes off it. She looks like the perfect conception of a mother. If we were going to create a time capsule for future dominant species of what a human mother looked like, this would be the first thing in.

I know, I said.

It's time to confront this, my wife said. It's time to face this thing head on.

She was right. For seventeen years I'd avoided my mother and her growing multimedia empire. She was everywhere still, on the news and the tabloids and the Internet and the movie screens, the highest paid actress in Hollywood, capable of carrying a movie on name alone. They were starting to get worse though, less artful and more popcorn-flickish. There were more explosions, more car chases, snippets of carefully-engineered and focus group tested dialogue.

We devoured all of it, my wife and me. We rented all of the movies and stayed inside for a solid week. I watched my mother's evolution from burgeoning actress to full-scale movie icon. When it got to be too much my wife took my hand in hers and reassured me.

Head on, she said. We have to hit this head on.

When the dust settled we'd consumed everything there was to consume. Four separate franchises. A handful of awful, artsy movies – including scenes that Mother should've never filmed – and another handful of uncredited cameos.

I thought we were done.

Then the buzz began. Mother had just finished a movie that was, according to one tabloid, going to "get her career back on track." The rumors were that she was going back to her roots and shedding the glam and glitz of the Hollywood structure.

I called my brother. We should go, I said to him. My wife thinks we need to take this thing head on.

Head on? my brother slurred drunkenly. What does that mean anyway? Like we should jump in front of a train?

No, I said. But we can't run from this thing forever. How's father?

Call him sometime, my brother said.

Maybe I will, I said.

All you'll get in response, he said, are moans and muffled cries.

The movie came out the following weekend. It was called ALL BETTER and the poster on the cineplex showed my mother pushing a cart with a full-grown man in the basket. The little boy with the cowlick all grown-up. He still wore his blue and red striped sweater and his cowlick was still intact.

Oh god, I said as my wife and I walked past it. I can't do this.

Head on, she said.

I relented. We walked into the cineplex and I got a drink and my wife some popcorn. She asked if I wanted any as we took our seats but my stomach was already flipping and flopping around inside my gut.

Calm down, she said. Your leg's moving a mile a minute.

This is a bad idea, I said.

It's the only way, she said, popping a kernel into her mouth.

The commercials and previews ran and then the feature started. The theater was full, maybe a hundred other people crowding my wife and me in. It started with the little boy with the cowlick, now a man with a cowlick, sitting in a little desk in a little classroom, surrounded by children who were obviously younger and smaller than him. A nervous smattering of laughter filled the theater.

Young man, the teacher, who looked suspiciously like an older Mrs. Blowings, at the chalkboard at the front of the class said, what're you doing over there?

The man with a cowlick was picking a single pencil at a time out of his desk and then ritually snapping them in two and letting them fall to the floor. He was obviously happy with this game until the teacher called upon him. Me? he asked. Nothing.

The laughter grew from nervous to full.

Wait, I whispered. That's not right.

My wife put her hand on mine again. Head on, she said.

But, I said.

Head on.

The man with a cowlick was punished and kept in from recess. The movie skipped forward to Mother picking him up from school. She was like Mother from then, with her dull hair and middle-class trappings, only she wasn't. There was an obvious lie to her appearance, a dissonance as if her celebrity self was trying to claw its way out from underneath all the prosthetics and make-up. The man with the cowlick got into the car with her and frowned.

You have a bad day? Mother asked him with fraudulent concern.

I had the worst day at school, the man with the cowlick said.

Oh, Mother said, what happened?

Teacher was mean to me, he said.

Hmm, Mother said and then looked right into the eye of the camera. Let's see what we can do about that.

My wife put her hand on my shoulder as I bristled. I turned to her and said, This is a lie. An out and out lie.

Honey, she said.

They went to the grocery store and Mother pushed an oversized cart that had been made to fit the man with the cowlick down the baking good aisles and then said, What would make it all better?

The crowd cheered and whistled. They could feel the story sprinting toward its inevitable conclusion.

Look at him, I screamed finally. He's a grown man. A grown man.

Honey, my wife said.

No, I said. He's a grown man.

The crowd was building to a froth and could not hear anything I was saying.

The man with the cowlick put his chubby, not-so-tiny fist against his chubby, not-so-tiny bubble cheeks and looked as if he were considering. This time though, it didn't take long. He knew his lines, knew what was expected from him. I want cupcakes, he said and the audience screamed the line right along with him.

All right then, Mother and the audience said simultaneously, cupcakes it is.

She reached for the box of cupcakes and the audience cheered wildly.

I wanted to leave but my wife pulled me back into my seat. Head on, she said again.

Honey, I protested. Please.

They were in the kitchen that was done up to look like the kitchen that was just a little bit nicer than the kitchen we had when I was little. The man with the cowlick was peeling the wrapper off his flawless cupcake and as it switched to my mother again, the pan of cupcakes in her hand, the same scene my poor brother had labored over trying to recreate, had tried to portrait in an attempt to win back my mother's plastic heart, I couldn't control myself any longer and launched myself out of my seat. My wife nearly followed me but chose instead to hide in the recesses of her chair.

I faced the delirious mass of an audience and pointed an accusing finger in their direction. This is a fraud, I screamed. A fraud if there ever was a fraud. But they didn't hear me. Their mouths were open as they were possessed of some nirvanic fervor that I could tell might never end, their faces nothing but the black holes of their mouths and rows of teeth. A fraud, I tried again, but was cut off as Mother, onscreen asked, All better?

The man with the cowlick took a bite and smiled. I turned and saw the crumbs cascading off his weathered face. He said, All better, but I couldn't hear it for the screaming from the audience, the rapturous chant now building into a mantra.

All better, they said.

All better, they said, my wife joining them.

I turned from the screen to them and then back to the screen. My mother was there, towering over me, sixty feet tall, the comfort of her once suburban face melting and twisting into something worse, something better, something I both recognized and something I knew nothing of.

MERCY, GIFT AND RAPTURE

Desi woke me in the late afternoon by turning the TV up full blast. She watched soaps all day every day and when I came to there was a plane rip-roaring through the sky. It was losing its engines and about to crash into the side of a mountain. A big fireball filled the screen as Desi put my steak and eggs on the kitchen table.

Oh no, she said as I rolled off the couch. There's three people on that plane.

Eh, I said and sat down in my chair. You know well as I do nobody dies for good in this shit.

No, she said. I guess they don't.

I cut in my steak, a gray-looking T-bone, and it was so rare blood leaked out and sogged up my eggs. It didn't matter though because I was so hung-over and a little bloody steak was known to do wonders. I gobbled it up and drank my coffee while Desi sifted through the paper and sighed.

If you're gonna sigh like that, I said, could you go in the other room?

Bill, she said, there's so much awful.

Course there is, I said. Course there is.

They're killin' all kinds of folks in Africa, she said.

They always are, I said, getting angry. Something had been lost for us, though I didn't know what it was.

Machetes and machine guns, she said.

As if on cue, Desi's cat Patton came sauntering in from the other room, his hair matted with snot. He was seventeen years old, barely going, and was Desi's parents' cat before they kicked off.

Hi Patty boy, Desi said, setting down her paper.

Patton let out a pathetic little cry and stumbled to the sink. Ever the bleeding heart, Desi picked him up and set him on the counter. She got the leftover eggs out of the microwave and put them in front of him. He more or less fell into those eggs and snorted and coughed until they were all gone.

Just save it, Desi said to me.

I'm not sayin' nothin', I said.

You thinkin' it though, she said.

I'm just sayin', I said, that if you love that cat you ought to have him put down. Show some mercy for once in your goddamn life.

Oh god, Desi said, that's awful.

Just then Patton took a weak step away from the bowl and fell to the floor.

Patty boy, Desi said. You okay?

He gave another half-assed meow.

He's sufferin', I said. Cat that old ain't nothin' but misery.

You can be so cold-hearted, she said to me and picked Patton off the ground. She held him in her lap like a baby doll and he looked like he'd run the hell away if he had the energy. He's part of the family, Desi said. That's no way to treat someone you love.

All right, I said. I'm gonna clean up and head out.

You just got up, she said as Patton finally escaped, and you're leavin' already?

Got things to do, I said, grabbing a beer out of the fridge for the shower.

After something of a fight I got in my truck and drove the five miles into town and parked in the lot for The Winding Way Bar & Grill. My buddy Gus managed it of the week and made sure the bartender got me my beer at gas station prices. There was no one there 'cept for a fella playing pool by his lonesome and I had my pick of seats at the bar.

Budweiser? the bartender asked.

Yessir, I said.

I polished it off quick. Then another. I was already feeling the old buzz flooding back when Gus came in and made a beeline for me.

Hey Gus, I said. What's the word?

Same bullshit, Gus said, different day.

I heard that, I said.

So, Gus said, I got some work to do, but you gonna be around awhile?

Think so, I said.

Okay, Gus said and let out a big gulp of air. Gus was a big guy, maybe three bills, and when he exhaled it was like an elephant breathing on you. I got someone wants to meet you, he said.

Someone wants to meet me? I said. Hot damn. This someone have a name?

Gus stared at me and then smiled. Katelyn, he said. Her name's Katelyn.

Katelyn, I said, like I was trying it on for size. Okay.

Gus smiled again and took off to do god knows what. I'd known the guy four years, since I made the move, and he'd always been kind. Sometimes he swung by and the two of us would down some beers and pop off a few rounds out back. He was good people, for sure, but I still didn't tell him anything about my past life.

It was a funny thing to carry so much shit around. One day you're set up for life in Illinois and the next you're driving off in the middle of the night and renting a place in Warsaw, Kentucky of all places. And the distance didn't help, no sir. I was still careful where I went and who I said what to.

But right then, at the bar, I wasn't worried about that. I had a belly full of Bud and I wasn't sweating Illinois or Desi or that damn cat or anything at all. I was thinking of Katelyn, who I'd never so much as seen but was in full and glorious love with. How Katelyn could've been anything but a big-tittied knockout with a love for literature I'd never know.

I tipped back another Bud and looked at the clock. Ten 'til seven. I imagined her walking in, big hips under a plaid skirt and even bigger boulders squeezed into a tank top. In my head she'd sit next to me and I'd say something smart about Sartre or Keats and the next thing I'd know she'd have my hand under the bar and trapped between her big thighs. By the time door got kicked in, I was asking her to run away in my dream. Asking her to come along and start things over again.

But the door got kicked in and when I looked around I noticed the bartender and that fella playing pool had all cleared out. Gus was nowhere to be found either. And the guy who walked in the door was a beast named Bower I knew from my previous life.

Blood, Bower said. Bloodbloodblood.

Hello old friend, said a voice from outside. I knew it was Teddy well before he stepped in, dressed in a cute little cream-colored suit.

Bower crossed the room in no time and got his paws around my neck. I was blacking out when he let go and Teddy's face was a few inches from mine.

You left Illinois in such a hurry, he said with a frown. We didn't even have a chance to say goodbye.

I was led out of the bar by Bower and tossed into the back of Teddy's green Jaguar. Before Bower got in the front seat he handcuffed me and slapped me so hard across the mouth that two of my teeth popped out and landed on the seat next to me.

You'll excuse the restraints, Teddy said, but we don't want you cutting this reunion short.

Teddy turned the key to the Jaguar and it hummed like a kitten. I'd been in that car so many times before, but never under that bad of circumstances.

Hey, Teddy said, pulling out onto the gravel road and flipping on the headlights. Bower, my good man, won't you give our friend here something to look at?

Bower grumbled and threw a handful of polaroids in my face. It was dark in the car, but I didn't have to look to know what they were. They were of Desi from years back in all manner of undress. Some of her in the shower, sopping wet. Some of her on a bed, showing me everything and teasing me nearer.

You recognize those? Teddy said.

I do, I said.

I thought maybe you did, he said. It'd be odd for such an accomplished photographer not to recognize his own work.

We drove in silence for the better part of twenty minutes, Teddy winding the Jaguar around the back roads and through the state forest. Every now and then Bower would get to breathing hard and he'd turn around and press his big gorilla-like face into the backseat and rain my cheeks with spit.

Bower's angry, Teddy said eventually. You see, Bill, he's a very reasonable man, Bower, and he doesn't like injustice. He doesn't like it when people take things that aren't theirs.

Who does? I said.

Bower reached back and drove the mountains of his knuckles into my chin and knocked my jaw out of place.

You're a funny man, Teddy said. A very funny man, Bill.

The car was silent again and I watched the headlights ahead of us bobbing through the dark. I could tell we'd entered the next county by how the signs had changed. We were heading, no doubt, for Berea, an hour or so away. I knew Teddy kept a safehouse there and if we got that far I was good as dead.

Maybe a half-hour outside Berea, Teddy said, I'll never forget the morning I woke up and she was gone. I'd had a dream that I was a fish and I was swimming upstream. The other fish were all coming at me, head-on, and when they hit me I could feel their scales and slime and I had to keep pressing forward.

Bone, Bower said. Motherfucking bone.

In due time, Teddy said to him. And when I made it upstream, Bill, do you know what I saw?

What? I said.

The bodies, Teddy said. All the bodies that I'd left in my wake.

I slumped back in the backseat and tried to work my hands out of the cuffs without any kind of success. I'd seen what Teddy and Bower were capable of. Had seen Bower bash a man's head in until all that was left was soup and bits of hair.

What happens now? I said.

What happens? Teddy said. Oh, nothing much Bill. We take you to a nice, safe place, we strap you to a bed, and we let Bower here live out all of his fantasies.

Bower turned around in his seat and gave a smile so big in the dark that his rocky yellow teeth glittered.

He's had dreams too, Teddy said. And in his dreams he removes a man's arms and legs and every last breathing organ until he simply disappears.

Bower reached into his pocket and pulled out the longest and sharpest skinning knife I'd ever seen.

It's a wonderful thing, Teddy said, when dreams come true.

I closed my eyes then and concentrated on my heart. The thing I wanted so bad right then was to reach in and make it stop. Dead cold stop. Turn it off like turning off a switch to a lamp. I said to it, Stop. Stop right now. And it just kept on beating. I gave up finally and opened my eyes and that's when I saw the deer.

Up ahead, in the middle of the road, a buck stepped out onto the centerline. It had a huge rack, maybe an eight-pointer, and it turned its head to us and watched the headlights race closer and closer. Teddy made the mistake most people do. He slammed on the brakes and wrenched the wheel of his Jaguar. The car went up on two wheels and then rolled over and over, three or four times, until we landed rightside up with a thud in a roadside ditch.

The front windshield was spidered through with cracks and splattered with blood from both the buck and Bower. Bower had rocketed forward when Teddy hit the brakes and the crown of his head bounced off the glass and caved in. He was sitting facedown against the console, his blood leaking out and onto the fine upholstered floor.

Teddy, from what I could tell, had been killed too. He didn't move, didn't seem to breathe, and when I yelled at him, Teddy, hey Teddy, he didn't budge. I was all right for the most part, maybe a broken rib or two, because I'd thrown myself in the seat just as soon as Teddy hit the brakes. I hurt bad as hell and blood was dripping down and stinging my eyes, but in a short I had my faculties back.

The first task was to get the cuffs off. I tried a trick an old buddy of mine had taught me where you rub one of your wrists against the metal until the skin starts to peel away. After a whole mess of blood and flesh was lost I could just barely slide my hand out. The door was dented in so far I had to lie back down on the seat, among the glass and blood, and mule kick until it finally flew out with a groan.

On the road, in the headlights, I could make out the deer that'd tumbled into the Jaguar and been thrown off the back end. Almost a perfect line from where it'd been hit. It lay there in the road, gurgling and hissing and moaning. Its back legs shattered, crooked at different, unnatural angles. One of its shiny black eyes caught mine and I thought of how lucky I'd been for that goddamn animal to step out and take a hit like that, and I thought about how I should do it a solid.

I went back to the Jaguar and knocked out the window where Bower was slumped over. The knife he'd showed me was on his lap and I reached in and got it. That was when I heard the noise from the driver's seat. Knife at the ready, I walked around and smashed that window too. Teddy couldn't look up, but he was breathing and moaning just like that deer.

How bad you got it? I said to him.

God, he said, oh god.

Teddy, I said. How bad you got it?

Bill, he said. Oh god, Bill.

I reached in and pulled him off the steering wheel. Glass caked his face and was sticking out of his cheek and lips and eyes. He was a mask of blood and gore and with every breath he moaned and whimpered.

Hey, I said. Teddy.

Bill, he said. Bill, oh god, it hurts. Oh god, I never knew.

You never knew such pain? I said.

No, he said. Oh god, Bill. No.

Good, I said and walked into the middle of the road. The buck was still struggling there, his broken legs running on their own. He let out a muzzled cry and I took that knife, Bower's knife, and ran it gently across his throat and let him go. The crying and the running stopped.

Teddy, I said from the road.

Yeah, he said mournfully.

You good in there? I said.

God, he said. Bill, he said. End me.

Visit again sometime, I said. We'll have us a reunion. A good one.

Bill, he said.

I got to get home to Desi, I said to him. Maybe we'll get the camera out for old time's sake.

Bill, he said as I walked away. Please.

I WANT YOU TO KNOW I WAS HERE

He woke from the dream and climbed down the stairs only to find her sitting there on his couch, among his things, oddly out of place, oddly comfortable. She said to him, I'm sorry.

Still trying to wake up and discern reality from dream he said to her, Sorry?

About sending the dream, she said. I'm sorry it had to be like that.

He kept his voice at a whisper. Upstairs his wife was sleeping. His son. He pointed at the door and said, I don't know what's going on, but you have to go.

I will, she said, but you have to know I was here.

You can't just show up in the middle of the night.

I've been here for days, she said. The South suits you.

You have to go, he said. Please.

Why?

My wife is upstairs.

And your boy.

And my boy.

What's his name? she said and shifted just so that the house was filled with the crack of the floor creaking.

Samuel, he said.

I'm glad it's old-fashioned, she said. I thought she would've wanted something modern, something that didn't sound right when it became Grandpa Such-and-Such.

Please go, he said. I'm going to have to call the cops. I mean it, he said. I have to tell you, I'm really thrown off here.

But you feel guilty.

A little.

Why?

I don't know, he said. But you need to leave.

You should know that I've been telling people I was pregnant with your baby for the last two years. I've lost all my friends because of it. My mother won't speak to me.

He placed his hand on the top of his bookcase that sat against the wall. There was a lamp there with some heft to it and he thought he might have to use it to protect himself. Please, he said. I keep asking you to leave.

If I try hard enough, she said, I can still feel him in there. The absence of him. The void. I imagine he's there now, learning his language and speaking to me in the middle of the night.

Please, he said.

I'm leaving. But I want you to know I was here.

I know, he said. Believe me, I know.

Then know this, she said. I know you.

You don't know me. It's been four years since I've even seen you, been in the same room. I'm different now.

I know you have the slightest speech impediment that no one else hears. Your accent hides it. All the Hoosier talk. I know when you were little you had ear infections and sometimes when you're nervous you hold your fingers at the base of your right ear and worry they'll come back.

Instinctively he touched the base of his ear. It occurred to him that these were the same words she'd spoken to him in the dream. In it he'd been in his bedroom, in his bed, and his phone had rang and when he answered it the voice on the other end was a woman's, a name he didn't recognize. She's been calling to tell him that this woman had been lying about being pregnant with his baby. That she was a liar. A witch.

Then the call had faded away and on the other end was her voice. The surprise was enough to set his teeth to grinding. I know you, she'd said. I know you have a speech impediment that no one else hears. All that Hoosier talk.

I don't know what to say to you, he said to her as she sat on his couch, as she ran her fingers over the pillows his wife had made, but you have to go.

Of course, she said and then sat the pillow aside and rose from her seat as if lifted by unseen hands. A lady always knows when it's time to take her leave.

For a moment he watched her walk to the door. Everything in him told him to let her leave, that it was a miracle she might go without disturbing his wife and child, but he felt his mouth opening and asking of its own accord, Did he have a name?

Calmly, she put fingers to the swell of her stomach. From where he was standing, from his place there in the near dark, he swore he could see it glow like palms pressed against the bulb of a flashlight. I just decided tonight, she said. Samuel is a fine, fine name.

TO THE END OF IT

They carried their rickety old lawn chairs down the walkway and onto the beach as the nanobots that had deposited themselves in their ears chirped, One hour until The Wave, one hour. The bots had been there for a week and had warned them every thirty minutes of the upcoming Wave. They had stopped wearing watches, everyone had, for how constant and unrelenting the alerts were.

I can't even begin to tell you how tired I am of these things, the woman said, planting her chair into the sand. I kept hoping they'd lay off after a few days and let us sleep.

The man brushed off his chair and said, I've started dreaming around it. Before speaking again he stared off into the waves of the ocean and sighed loudly. Every dream I have now has that voice in it. That artificially sweet voice.

She said, You've started talking in your sleep. You've started saying, in the middle of the night, three days and four hours until The Wave.

That's awful, he said.

It is awful.

Between them was the picnic basket the man had carried and the woman opened the top and pulled from it two plastic glasses and a bottle of wine. The cork was already popped and now sat halfway out the mouth of the bottle. The woman poured the man a glass and then one for herself.

Offering a toast, the man said, To the end of it.

The woman tapped her plastic glass against his and was disappointed by the lack of a clinking sound. To the end, she said, a note of somberness in her voice.

Do you remember, he asked, that night on Tybee Island?

The woman smiled. Of course she remembered. Hardly a month went by when she didn't actively try and clutch hold of those memories. They'd rented a cottage three blocks away from the beach and one night, after sharing a few bottles of cabernet sauvignon, they'd walked hand-in-hand to the water and made love in the waiting arms of a lifeguard stand.

We were trying to decide if we should stay together or not, she said.

Do you regret that? he asked her. The decision?

She thought of the discussion, the huddled, quieted argument under the low lights of a local crab shack. There was a man playing guitar on a stool on the tiny stage in the corner. It was a Jim Croce song. Maybe Cat Stevens. The two of them had been nearing an agreement to say goodbye, to go their separate ways.

You said we should take the night and sleep on it, she said.

And then we went to the beach, he said.

She offered her glass and this time he reciprocated.

Forty-five minutes until The Wave, the bot squeaked in their ear.

If I could pull it out I would crush it, the man said.

The woman took a sip and laughed quietly. You try all the time.

I dig and I dig and I dig, but it's so tiny.

Kathleen said she read somewhere they're no bigger than a grain of sand.

That's what I heard, the man said. Then: Say, what are her and Roy doing? Did they make a decision?

She wasn't sure, the woman said before finishing her glass. She filled it again and blew a long stream of air. Kathleen told me they're still figuring it out, but you know Roy. He's so nervous all the time. He's scared of his own shadow. Kathleen said he's been terrified of dying ever since he was a little boy.

Aren't we all? the man said.

You're afraid?

Petrified. Aren't you?

I don't know, she said. I've been spending a lot of time trying to nail down what I'm feeling.

And?

I think I'm afraid, she said, but I'm a little relieved.

The man reached for the bottle of wine and filled up his glass. By the faint light of the stars the woman watched him swirl the liquid. Relieved, he said.

I can't explain it, she said. I couldn't begin to.

There was quiet then as they watched the black form of the ocean roll over the horizon and listened to the soft rustling of the waves. The next voice they heard was the bot telling them there was thirty minutes left.

Damn it, the man said.

I guess that's what I mean, she said. I won't have to hear it anymore. I won't have to listen to that damn thing in my ear. It'll shut off.

What if it's just quiet?

What?

Everything, he said. After you're gone. What if it's just quiet? Blackness and quiet.

I guess I wouldn't mind that, she said. I guess I could handle that.

That's what scares me, he said. I get where Roy's coming from. If it's nothing, if it's just blackness and quiet, I think I'd go insane.

But honey, she said, you wouldn't be aware. There'd be no *you* to go insane.

He took a swig. It gives me the creeps.

Careful, she said. We need to save a little.

Sure, he said.

Do you remember what you said to me? she asked. When we were in that stand? On the beach?

Sure, he said.

Say it again, she said.

Stay with me forever, he said. That's what I said.

I'll never forget that. Just thinking about it gives me chills.

In the dark she felt his hand reach hers and their fingers intertwine.

Stay with me forever? he said.

Quickly she let go. That's a cruel joke, she said.

What?

At a time like this. You know what that means.

I'm sorry, he apologized. I thought that's what you wanted to hear.

I did, she said. I guess I don't know what I want.

Fifteen minutes, the bot said.

So, he said, should we get to it?

The woman tipped her glass just so the wine trickled down and barely brushed her lips. She savored the light touch of flavor and said, I suppose we should.

The man reached back into the picnic basket. When his hand returned to her vision he had in his palm a small canvas bag and when it was opened he held two white pills that seemed to glimmer in the dark.

One for you, he said and handed the woman one.

How long do they take to work? she asked him.

Five minutes. Tops.

And where'd you get them?

They were handing them out in town. They said they didn't want anybody joining who didn't want to.

That's comforting, she said.

At least they're honest. Not really the time to lie, I guess.

Are you going to take yours?

Are you?

She hesitated before saying, Yes. Are you?

Yes, he said.

One, two, three?

One, two, three.

All right, she said. One.

Two, he said.

Ten minutes, the voice tweeted, this time like a bird.

The man huffed. Damn it, he said again.

Okay, she said. Down the hatch.

The two of them placed the shining white tablets on their tongues and took a drink of their wine. Once they had swallowed they turned to each other and held hands.

With resignation, he said, That's that.

I love you, she said.

I love you too.

Have you always?

Always, he said.

So have I. Even when times were rough. Even when we were thinking of saying goodbye.

And you don't regret the decision? he asked.

No, she said and squeezed his hand. Never.

Me either.

Good.

Five minutes, the voice whispered.

Shouldn't it be working? she said.

I'm getting tired, he said. I think it's working.

I'm getting tired too, she said.

Good, he said. If it's not nothing, he said, find me?

I will, she said, feeling her eyelids growing massively heavy with each passing breath. You find me?

Always, he said as if he were drifting off.

She closed her eyes and remembered again how he had held her on the beach so many years before. The air had been warm on her bare skin and she breathed in its salt and the salt from his slick body. All of the fighting seemed so far away then, like something that had happened to somebody else, a disagreement they'd overheard in a bar one night. None of it made sense, none of it felt real or pressing or relevant anymore. She wanted to hold that peace again, live in it forever, swim in a great black sea of tranquility and never ever come up for air.

It seemed possible then, like she'd entered a new reality where nothing stretched on forever and held her in its arms and rocked her like a blind and deaf child. It was an amity that felt stranger and more exhilarating for her than any moment or second of her entire life.

But still, she searched for him.

She groped blindly through the lightless ocean, her hands, her fingers, her skin searching through shadows upon shadows upon shadows. It was a search that lasted days, weeks, months, years, lifetimes. One existence after another rolling and twirling and mingling and fumbling for him.

Then, the darkness receded like a flood run its course.

Light. White-hot light.

The voice returned. Only now it wasn't a grain of sand in her ear.

It wasn't a chirp or even saccharine sweet.

It was her own voice.

The Wave, she found herself saying, is complete.

Like blinds, her eyelids opened with a shock and she was staring out into the ocean, the waves glinting black and white under some midnight sun. The world was robbed of color as each rise and crest sparkled like a sea of circuits, a mass of machinery rolling and toiling. The sand at her feet a web of motherboards and interconnected circuits. Blinking electric eyes. Veins of organic metal.

She raised her hand and saw her skin now seemed almost like diamond, like quartz, the knuckles of her fingers hubs and elbows of brass. It was as if sleet had razed the land and peppered it with violent metal in lieu of ice.

With a great grinding of gears, she turned slowly to see the man staring back at her. Gone were the soft curves of his body, the face she remembered and loved so well from that night spent as squatters on the beach. Replacing them a beehive of pulsing and electric processors, a colony of microchips grouped like schematics for a sprawling and lonely city.

Please, he said to her, eyes shining like mad and violent stars as his voice was routed and rerouted through an infinity's worth of synthesizers, asking, pleading, Stay with me forever?

CARRY WHAT YOU CAN KILL

In the Summer of Ninety-Three the woods in Brown County were pregnant with all variety of deer. The pests swelled out of the trees and into neighboring yards and roads and ate and fornicated over all manner of things. Does with new offspring harassed the elderly and puffed up against windows and snorted with rage and contempt for anybody unlucky enough to cross their paths. Put four people in the hospital in a two-week span. Ruined crops and upset the natural order of things. Newspaper announced not long after that the DNR was calling for open season under a headline that read *Carry What You Can Kill.*

Soon every idiot with a twenty-two and a pocketful of shells descended and got to killing. You couldn't blame them. Not really anyway. It was free meat, the chance to store up for a few years. That's what I had in mind anyway. My brother Joe worked at the rent-to-own place on Bethel and I had money down on some freezers. With his discount it would've been dumb not to buy a whole garage's worth. Seemed like the economical thing to do, butcher up some meat and keep my family in venison and sell the rest for profit.

Before I left I told my wife I loved her and took care to let her know she needed to get my son under control by the time I got back. He was willful, a degenerate comprised of rage and hatred and just enough know-how to do some damage. Ten years old and he'd already held a pair of scissors to my oldest daughter's throat and threatened to cut until his arm wore out. The two of us had had our fair share of rows and I'd grown tired.

Get him straightened out, I said to my wife, or he'll be on one of those hooks.

She knew what I meant. Out in the garage I had a whole system of hooks and hangings in place to drain the blood from the deer. Called it the Butcher Shop. My wife, as sensitive in her ways as my son was cold, hated to venture in there.

It's barbaric, she said, tugging at the fabric of her white linen dress.

One person's barbarism, I said, is another's art.

When I left the first morning with Trigger, my best friend from childhood, the boy was peering out the window. He'd lost a chunk of his cheek in a fishing accident and the scar was bubbling with infection and redness. His adam's apple bobbed crazily up and down his neck while I threw the truck in reverse. Our eyes locked and I knew better than to take my gaze from his.

Weakness was not a trait either of us tolerated.

Outside the woods the parking was at a premium and all the hunters sat in the back of their trucks, drinking beer and cleaning their weapons. The air smelled of fire and oil. Someone that morning had jumped the gun and got a stud in a thicket and dragged his body to the parking lot. It lay there on the gravel, flies swooping in and out of the cool air and landing in the emptied chest cavity. The stench rose up and mixed with the fire and oil. Children in orange hats poked its hide with the muzzle of their toy rifles and smiled while their father's snapped pictures with disposable cameras.

Fuck, Trigger said to me. We'll be lucky if we get out of here alive.

He had a point. From my count there were at least six dozen idiots in the parking lot and most looked like hobbyists, the kind of amateurs who would unload both barrels on anything that moved.

Knowing that most would prefer to stay within a half-mile of the parking lot, I told Trigger we'd go deep. It seemed like elementary reasoning, penetrating into the heart of the woods and setting up camp where few dared to go.

Bucks've already razed it, Trigger said. Probably nothing left but some sticks and a few blades of grass. Fuck all, he said.

I looked into the eye of the woods and saw the trees multiplying into the distance. At the center of it all was green, lush canopy and the chittering of birds and squirrels. There was life there, and when I told Trigger as much he shrugged his shoulders and unloaded his favorite shotgun and a bag full of pistols.

Pistols won't kill a deer, I said.

I gestured at the other men. Ain't for the deer.

At the stroke of seven a.m. they unleashed us. Bobby Piggsley, the DNR officer we all called Hog, strolled out from behind the wheel of his pick-up and said we had seventy-two hours to do whatever we wanted. Hog wasn't one to mince words. No tagging, no bagging, he said. Clear those motherfuckers out and we'll go home and have ourselves a time.

The rush was unlike anything I'd ever seen before. We were shoulder to shoulder for the first hundred yards and already there were crowds of game darting through the trees. Looking back you could still see the cars and trucks in the lot, Hog standing there sipping coffee out of a styrofoam cup, and yet there they were: deer. Emaciated, desperate, wild-eyed deer. Bobbing between trunks and rushing down and into the valley of the forest floor. Down there: more deer. A swarming like the cloud of gnats above that hollowed-out carcass. Bashing into each other, slipping and falling and being trampled.

Then came the shots. Fellas everywhere unleashing their weapons, the series like a thousand M-80's meeting their fuse. It blistered my eardrums and yet I found it in me to pull my trigger as well. Someone somewhere let loose an arrow and it sailed through the air above us. I watched it hit a buck in the shoulder and the buck stumbled and burrowed its rack into the dirt. Another arrow came. Another. More shots. Powder from the next man over burned my eyes.

I found Trigger. He had stayed back a ways, shouldered his gun. Blood caked his hands. He was smoking one of the small cigars he loved so well. I've already got more than I did the whole of last season, he said.

We've been here five minutes.

I know, he said and I followed his gaze. The herd was flowing in and over itself in the panic, like a nest of newborn snakes humping one another in their blindness. A wave of men was rushing them, knives drawn, stabbing wildly at whatever came near, some of the bucks twisting in their agony and baring their points. The men whooped and hollered, saying nonsense things, shouts about their childhood and places gone and things seen. Then the words turned to sounds, grunts and hisses. My stomach, Trigger said, is a boiling pot of water. But I can't look away.

The air stunk of powder and copper. The blood drenched the ground and formed puddles and it got so bad you had to watch your step as you climbed down into the bowl of the valley to collect your kill. We gave up responsibility, choosing instead to grab whatever buck or doe was nearby and dragging it out by its neck and up onto higher ground. Men patted each other on the backs, leaving dark red prints on their camoed jackets. One here or there rubbed a blood-streaked hand across his face and let it dry to war paint. The heart of the bowl a stumbling, steaming mess. We threw our cleanings there and the pile grew so large it almost shouldered us out of the valley altogether. All the small creatures of the forest gathered at the edge and waited their turns. The children who had come with their fathers frolicked and took potshots at the squirrels and raccoons and grabbed them by their hides and bashed them together.

It reminded me of my son. The one and only time I had taken him hunting had been a mistake, a bad exercise in brutality. When he saw a fawn drinking from a stream he had dropped his rifle, the one that'd belonged to his grandfather, his birthright, and taken chase. It wasn't a quarter mile into the line of trees that he'd caught it, wrestled it to the ground, and gouged out its eyes and shoved his hand into its slit of a mouth. I tried to pry him from the poor young thing, fumbling at the same time to draw my weapon so I could show it mercy, but my son, only seven at the time, was already mess of feral muscle. He strangled the fawn, beat its head against an outcropping of stone, and dug his nails so deep into its hide that they burst through. Before burying it beneath a pine on the other side of the creek, I had to beat the boy until he left it alone. There was anger in him though, a lust that'd been woke, for he leapt at me and crawled up the front of my jacket and butted his head against my chin. I sensed he aimed to kill me as well so I threw him as hard as I could to the ground and worked the heel of my boot against his tiny throat. Son of mine, I said, life is snuffed out so easily.

That night Trigger and I made camp a good two miles in. There were still deer poking about, their eyes wide in terror. Trigger had taken to firing pot shots at them, warnings. Occasionally he'd hit one and it would whimper and sprint away. We had a basic tent pitched in a clearing and we cuts lengths of steak and cooked them over a small fire. In the distance we heard the cheering of men. The occasional rifle shot that soon coalesced into a storm of discharges.

Trigger was quiet as he cut his steak with his hunting knife. He was glaring into the heart of the fire. I asked him what he was thinking and he shrugged. You ever reckon you'd see something like this?

No sir.

A young buck tiptoed up to the fire and smelled our plates. He wasn't the least bit frightened or intimidated. I could tell he was from the new breed of animal that'd taken hold, the ones that sprinted into the neighborhoods and attacked anything unlucky enough to exist in their path. The ones with full-awareness of death and all its intricacies, and yet seemingly unimpressed.

Shoo, Trigger said to him. Go on and shoo.

The buck snarled his lip and puffed out of his wet black nose.

Trigger retrieved his pistol from under leg and leveled it and cocked the hammer. Now, he said, his voice growing firmer, you go on and shoo.

The buck lowered his head like he might try and gore Trigger and then, as if the thought had only occurred to him, shifted and trotted off into the woods at a calm pace. There was another symphony of fire not far off. A lone man chuckled and soon the chuckle infected his party and they stood laughing like pleased dogs.

Only thing that seems to matter anymore, Trigger said, dumping what was left of his steak in the fire, is that a man can feed himself and only himself.

Trigger lifted himself off the forest floor and dusted off his pants. There was blood caked in the thighs of his jeans and whatever joy had been on his face that morning seemed forgotten. He excused himself to the tent and I stood watching the piece of meat sizzle in the flames.

Not long after I joined him and found him fully awake with his hands under his head. I found my spot and between his shallow breathing and the far-off shots, I found peace enough to slip under. It was a fitful sleep full of starts and lulls, but sometime in the night I found my way to dream and dreamed of that buck that'd wandered into our camp. I saw him in the company of his herd, his mouth boiling with spit and taste for a new meat. He lowered that new rack of his and set forth butting and piercing with wild abandon, goring until his neck couldn't stand the impact anymore and he was forced to rear up and then continue with his sharp hooves. All around him were the cries of his own and they snapping their heads to and fro and looking to each other in dumb wonder as to how such a massacre could ever visit them.

In the middle of the night I woke with a start. I had sweated through my clothes. Trigger was still awake, still staring at the steeple of the tent. Trigger, I said.

I know, he said. Go home.

As fast as I could I slipped on my boots and hurried off in the direction of my truck. Just a ways off was the pile of bounty I'd procured. They lay in twisted heaps, surrounded by starving animals. What was left of the glint of the fire played off their black eyes and I saw specks of light dance and then die. Under my breath, I apologized and sprinted through the woods.

The first mile was quiet, the sky overhead a muted ink-blue and the trees illuminated enough so that I never had to break stride. Then I came to the eye of the woods and the world became black. Good sense told me to stay, to wait for the hint of dawn, but I knew I had to get home. It grew quiet until the quiet grinded at me and then the quiet broke as a bullet hissed by. A tree only three feet away welcomed it and I heard the pulp of the wood sigh as if in relief.

Not a deer, I yelled. Not a deer.

There was the sound of a pair of men conferring. Then laughter. Laughter like a child's. Doesn't matter, one of them said. Doesn't make one lick of a goddamn difference.

I took off full-bore and held my hands out at a distance so that if I came across a tree I'd at least have a chance of surviving. There was one more shot, a wild one that missed by at least a dozen feet. There was more laughing, more conferring. And then nothing.

The parking lot was still alive in a limping manner. There were men stretched from car to car, their backs against the doors, makeshift fires dying at their feet. Everywhere there were piles of bodies stacked like loose and rotting bricks. Hog was leaned against one of them, drinking coffee and bullshitting. I tell you, he said as I rushed by, I could get used to this shit.

Sitting at the bumper of my truck was a group of men drunken and mumbling. One of them, a white-bearded man, the sleeve of his right arm folded and pinned up by what was left of his bicep, looked up at me with cataract eyes. Morning, boss, he said to me. Morning.

Home was twenty minutes away. I made it in ten, the cab of my truck stinking of blood and when I caught a glimpse of myself in the mirror it was like a glimpse of man come home from war.

As I carried my rifle out of my truck, I found the first of the bodies in the front yard. My middle-daughter. She'd been fond of paper dolls, of playing out scenes with her characters, her children she called them, and by her mutilated hand lay the one she was fond of most of all. Peggy, she called it, a young girl with short hair colored red by crayon.

A few feet from her was the oldest and then the youngest, lain out like boot prints and discarded like litter.

My wife was slumped on the bottom of the stairs. The white linen dress she'd been wearing that morning soaked through like an amateur had tried to stain it. Next to her, on the stair, the pair of scissors the boy had taken a liking to. I kicked them away and they went skittering down the floor. The sound must've roused him as I heard movement just past the door that led into the garage. I put my hand to my beloved's cheek and felt the cold already sunk in.

In my garage I found him sitting with his naked heels pressed together, the glimmer of his sweat-soaked body shining in the soft light from the moon. The nest of hooks and chains swung softly overhead, their metal playing a tune of discord and violence. He was staring up into them and smiling like a child filled with the most innocent of wonder. They rustled, seemingly on their own accord, and the pink gash that had grown from his cheek to trail and infect most of his face, winked at me in the dark.

Father, he said, you're home.

THE MOMENT BEFORE THE EARTH WAS DESTROYED

Before humanity was destroyed the aliens paused time and took Tex Halders aside. He was standing in a parking lot in Houston when the sky paused. The traffic paused. The neon light at the Hard Rock Café across the street paused. The aliens approached Tex and told him the score. All human life has been paused and will be destroyed in short order, this said in their hive-voice. We'd like a tour and we've chosen you to be our guide.

Why me? Tex said.

Why not? they said.

You've got a point, Tex said.

Everything everywhere was paused. Monster truck races. Twinkie factories. High-fructose corn syrup distilleries. Marketing firms.

What do you want to know? Tex asked the aliens.

Well, the aliens said, take us through the whole of human achievement. Before we destroy we like to know. For ages and ages we've observed. It's been quite informative, but we'd like to have our questions answered.

All right, Tex said, ask away.

Why war? the aliens said. Why genocide?

Hell, Tex said, I don't know. At some point you got to start killing.

The aliens looked at each other. The answer didn't seem satisfactory to them. But, they said, why war?

Listen, Tex said, if you're gonna ask questions I'm gonna give you answers. If you don't like 'em, then go screw off.

All right, the aliens said. That's fair. Tell us then, they said, what about art?

You've got the wrong guy, Tex said. I don't know fuck-all about art.

What about Van Gogh? they said. Picasso? Pollock?

Here's what I know about art, Tex said. I know sometimes there are pictures of flowers in my hotel rooms. You want to know about pictures of flowers in hotel rooms, I'm your man.

What of the great books? they said. Explain them to us. Explain literature. Explain philosophy.

Tex was tired. The sun, frozen like everything else in existence and suspended overhead, was beating down. Hey, he said, I get that you're curious, but hell, it's hotter than a fat boy's crotch out here.

Fine, the aliens said. What about this?

They took Tex to another quadrant of the parking lot where a steel gray minivan was parked. One of the aliens motioned his hand under the rear bumper and the hatch opened on its own.

Oh, Tex said, that's an easy one. Let's say you just got done shopping at the Target. Say you got an armload of groceries. He pantomimed like he was carrying an armful of sacks. All right, he said, you can't reach out and open the hatch, right? He moved his foot under the bumper and the hatch opened again. Open sesame, he said.

Interesting, the aliens said in their hive mind. Utility. Common sense.

That's right, Tex said.

The pinnacle of human achievement, they said.

You bet your ass, Tex said.

Fine, they said. Thank you, they said and blinked the Earth out of existence.

EVERYTHING THAT BLOSSOMS

You always said I had a problem with happy endings. That whenever my narratives got near the end they started to spoil like coddled milk. You were the optimist, the one who looked at the uneven and crooked pictures on the wall and said their imperfections gave you something to do tomorrow, something to live for.

I tried to argue, standing in the living room, shouting as you cuddled under a quilt with Duke, our old and chubby basset hound. I said the rule of the universe was entropy. Death and destruction.

You just shook your head. What you're not seeing, you'd say, is the beauty of it. The rising buildings. The walls. The ceilings. The way it all grows and blossoms.

But those walls will tumble. Those ceilings cave in. Everything that grows must die and everything that blossoms must wither.

You were never convinced. Here, you said, handing me a sheet of paper. Write me a story. Write me a happy ending.

Duke had sloughed his way off the couch and taken a seat on my toes. Once, when I was in one of my states and obsessing over dying, you told me you knew I wasn't because he wasn't worrying over me, wasn't nursing me with attention. I wrote: *Duke was born without a name and with a mother who couldn't recognize him. He grew old and white in the muzzle. He died and was buried under the pine tree in the backyard.*

When I handed it to you I expected a shaking of the head. I expected you to crumple the paper and toss it in the corner. Instead, you leapt from the couch. Here, you said, framing the story with your fingers on my desk and then narrowing them until only *He grew old and white in the muzzle* was left. There it is, you said. You found it.

THE AUTHOR

Jared Yates Sexton is a born-and-bred Hoosier living and working in Georgia as an Assistant Professor of Creative Writing at Georgia Southern University. He is the author of *An End To All Things*, *The Hook and The Haymaker*, and *Bring Me The Head of Yorkie Goodman*.

NOW AVAILABLE FROM

forget me/hit me/let me drink great quantities of clear, evil liquor
By Katie Schmid

The State Springfield Is In
By Tom C. Hunley

The Hook and The Haymaker
by Jared Yates Sexton

What to Do When You're Buried Alive
By Michael Meyerhofer

For more info about the press and our titles, please visit:

www.splitlippress.com
www.twitter.com/splitlippress
www.facebook.com/splitlippress
www.splitlippress.wordpress.com

AND DISCOVER MORE IN

Find great literature, music, fine art and film by visiting:

www.splitlipmagazine.com
www.facebook.com/splitlipmagazine
www.twitter.com/splitlippress

www.ingramcontent.com/pod-product-compliance
Lightning Source LLC
Chambersburg PA
CBHW020650260626
47157CB00008B/2982